CARRY ME THROUGH CHRISTMAS

RACHEL HOLM

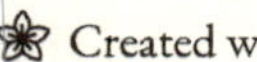 Created with Vellum

To my Dad, for giving me his love of Christmas, with enough left over to want to share that love with the world.

Chapter 1

March

Blaire

You know how they always say you can't go home again? I've never actually believed that. Coming home again to Holly Ridge to head up the Christmas festival has always been my plan, my dream, what I've been working toward, but I never imagined it would be like this.

I walked up the front steps to city hall, pausing for a moment to take a deep breath before reaching for the brass door handle attached to one of the stately oak double doors, making sure my sensible pencil skirt, flats, and blazer were straight and neat and steeled myself for what was ahead. I had paired my standard business armor with my favorite blue shirt that had the double impact of being my favorite color and making my eyes pop. A little power suit and power color combo. Even if I was feeling all jumbled up inside, I was sure to present a powerful front.

I opened the door and my eyes immediately found the row of pictures of past mayors on the left-hand side of the entry hall. Among those pictures was the picture of Dad, mayor of Holly Ridge for twenty-five years before he retired five years ago. I was intentional in not letting my eyes land on the photos of the City Council—created in a change to town governance structure after Dad's retirement—on the right-hand side of the entry hall. They were the reason this homecoming wasn't as joyous as I imagined.

I walked up a short set of stairs and smiled at Larry, the city hall security guard, who had known me since I was a little girl coming to visit Dad at work. "If it isn't the prodigal daughter, back to save the day," Larry greeted me.

"Saving the day is what Greenes do in this town, Larry." I responded with a confidence I wasn't sure I completely felt.

Fake it till you make it, right?

I continued down the long hall to the Alder conference room, where my soon-to-be bosses had indicated I should meet them. Taking one more deep breath, I took in the three individuals sitting on one side of the table, heads together in conversation. Rudolph, the council president, with an unfortunate red nose—*I wish I was kidding*—sat in the middle. Agatha, a stern-looking woman, sat on his right, and Arthur, Agatha's twin brother, sat on his left. Their conversation ceased as I entered the room. I moved to take a seat across from them and pulled out my notebook, ready to get this meeting started.

Rudolph cleared his throat. "Thank you for meeting with us today, Blaire. As Mondays are some of the busiest days for the town council, we'll jump right in."

I restrained my scoff with a slight smile I knew didn't reach my eyes. From my understanding, Mondays were only busy because the council refused to take appointments any other day of the week. Instead, I simply replied, "Looking forward to it."

Rudolph continued. "As you know, we hired you to take over running the Holly Ridge Christmas Festival this year. The festival's fund has shrunk significantly over the past several years, and if this year's festival isn't a success, it could mean the end of the Christmas festival for this town."

I shuddered internally. "Yes, I'm aware of the situation.

Agatha was kind enough to forward me the financials so I would know what I was working with in terms of a festival budget before signing my contract."

Arthur jumped in at this point. "Ah, yes, your contract. Did you bring it with you?"

I hadn't expected to need to use so much restraint so quickly, but perhaps I shouldn't have been surprised given how much disdain I held for the three people sitting across from me.

"Of course, I have it here." Reaching into my bag and pulling out the detailed and extensive contract the council's lawyers had apparently felt was necessary to lock in a festival planner, I handed the contract across the table. Even if the contract seemed unnecessarily complex, I knew I would have signed any document that brought me home to work on the Christmas festival. Even if some of the terms about finishing out the planning and preparation for this year, regardless of financial or oversight changes, had seemed a little extreme.

"Excellent," Rudolph responded. "Unfortunately, the Chief Financial Officer from Winterberry Glen wasn't able to be present with us today, so the next thing you're going to want to do is make an appointment to meet with him to talk about next steps for the festival planning process."

It took a moment for that to sink in, my brain short-circuiting as I asked, "Wait, what?! Why is someone from Winterberry Glen working with me on our festival?"

"Well, actually," Arthur continued, pushing those glasses firmly back onto the bridge of his nose, where they were determined to not stay, "a more accurate description is that someone from Winterberry Glen will be supervising your work and approving budgetary expenditures."

This didn't help things make any more sense.

"Okay," I said, "that seems to be splitting some technical hairs, but again, the question is why?"

Rudolph's cheeks flushed red to match his nose.

"Well, Blaire, it's like this. Not only does the future of the Christmas festival rest on the success of this year's planning, but the future of the town does too."

For a moment, I was too stunned to speak. Then, with a panicked edge to my voice, I exclaimed, "What does *that* mean?!"

"What it means," Agatha responded, "is that the festival funds are not the only funds that are depleted. The entire town budget is in the red. If the town defaults on its budget one more time, the state is going to disenfranchise the town and merge it with Winterberry Glen. As part of that process, the finance officer from Winterberry Glen must be involved in all major town spending decisions, so we can limit the damage to the financial future of the newly incorporated area if the towns are combined. I assume the . . . unpleasant history between Holly Ridge and Winterberry Glen won't be a problem for you, given the stakes."

Speechless wasn't a state I found myself in often, but here I was, absolutely and positively at a loss for words. I couldn't believe that in the five years since the town council had taken over, things had really gotten this bad. Of course, I had heard rumblings that infrastructure projects were going unmet and that school funding had been cut. But that was happening everywhere. How in the world could the future of the town have come to this? These buffoons had taken control of our town, and apparently, ruined everything.

"How is this the first I'm hearing about this?"

Arthur answered. "It's been kept under wraps, but now that you've been told as the planner of the Christmas festival, a press-release is going out today. Soon everyone will know that you're the last hope to save Holly Ridge."

The unfairness of this statement hit me in waves. Why in the world ha' the council let the town's budget problems get so bad that we were to the point of *needing* a last hope? I opened my mouth to say as much, but Rudolph, Arthur, and Agatha were exiting the conference room, leaving me to sit alone in stunned silence.

"Welcome home, indeed," I murmured to myself as I made the trek back to my parent's house, where I was staying until I could locate a rental of my own in Holly Ridge. Now it seemed like I might end up staying with them longer term, if I wasn't guaranteed to be here longer than the rest of the year. I had started to count my chickens, assuming my contract would be easily renewed following a successful festival.

I barely noticed the familiar and comforting scenery of my beloved hometown as it crawled past my windows, the same houses and landmarks that I'd known my whole life blurring into nothing more than background noise as I contemplated the task in front of me.

"C'mon, Blaire, plan a spectacular Christmas festival to save the whole town! How in the world am I supposed to pull that off?!" I said to myself.

I had been working my entire adult life toward the goal of coming back home and running the Christmas festival. Everyone had assumed I would just coast off my Dad's coattails when it came to getting a job, so I set out to prove them wrong. I didn't want to get the job through those connections. I wanted to get the job because I was the best for it. So, after college, I found myself in other small towns around the tristate area working on their festivals and special events, gaining experience and credentials to return home with. It turned out I was fantastic at what I did, succeeding in growing any festival I had worked on, and navigating small-town politics was something I was born to do, but none had stakes like this before. I had never been in charge by myself before either, there was always someone I had to answer to, who would try to take credit for my successes. It looked like that wouldn't be any different in this scenario either, with Winterberry Glen's CFO having to sign-off on almost everything I do, but at least I could count on him not trying to take credit for Holly Ridge-related successes thanks to the town feud. I'd just have to watch out for sabotage instead, which was definitely something I had experienced before. To say I was wary of men who worked in government would be an understatement. Not everyone was honorable and transparent like my dad, a lesson I learned the hard way.

I was returning to Holly Ridge and the festival ahead of schedule—this is what I get for not looking a gift horse in the mouth. I thought I was being recruited because of the reputation I had built for growing and succeeding in those other towns, but it was really because the council knew I was the only sucker loyal enough to this town with a chance in hell of pulling it off successfully. I'm not sure if that stung more than a nepotism hire right out of college would have or not.

My thoughts returned to the town. Once word got out the town's future was in danger, an even bigger blow for people would be that the consequence of failure was being absorbed by Winterberry Glen. The animosity between Holly Ridge and Winterberry Glen was not something that I had ever understood. Whenever I had encountered anyone from Winterberry Glen over the years, usually at the Wally World that was located at our towns' borders, they had seemed just like anyone from Holly Ridge, but the bad blood was strong and deep for most people in our town. I made a mental note to visit the archives at the library to read up on the feud. I could sense a research project resulting in color coded notes in my future. This just added an extra layer of complications to what seemed to be an already impossible scenario.

Parking my car in my parent's driveway, I steeled myself for the onslaught of sights and sounds that would await me. My dad was embracing his retirement with both hands, and though my mom had never worked outside the home, her joy at having her favorite companion home all the time radiated through the air. Throw in my niece and nephew, who my parents watched during the day when they weren't in school, and it was a whole host of energy I wasn't sure I was prepared to face after the sneak-attack meeting I had just endured. At least my sister would still be at work, saving me from the internal comparison I couldn't help but make between our lives. I had been focused more on accomplishing a career goal than on adding to the family's roster with my own husband and family, while she had managed to do both.

"Auntieeee Blaire!"

A blur of limbs and blond hair charged down the hall toward me as soon as I opened the door, and my niece, Holland, launched herself at me. Dropping my bag just in time, I relished her quick cuddle until she started wriggling, demanding to be put down to rejoin her partner in crime and twin brother, Hollis, back in the kitchen. The entry hall was lined with the Greene family photo museum, many photos featuring the very festival that had just been dropped in my lap like the hot potato from hell, with one terrifying expiration date attached.

"Blaire, is that you?" My mom called to me from the kitchen, where I saw she was elbows deep in flour when I rounded the corner.

"Yes, Mom. I do hope Holland isn't in the habit of greeting strangers off the street with that sort of enthusiasm."

My mom smiled at me good-naturedly, knowing my snark was all for show. With her greying hair in a neat bob, and the blue eyes I had inherited from her twinkling, I knew she was fully in her element—baking with the grandkids.

Just then, the back door opened and my dad walked into the kitchen from the backyard where he was no doubt tinkering in his workshop—and maybe hiding a bit from the overwhelming kid energy that had taken over the house during their spring break. Though dad was supposed to be "taking it easy" now that he was retired, he had the spring in his step of a much younger man, with shining green eyes and a salt-and-pepper beard to match his hair.

My parents had bought this house thirty-five years ago when my sister was a toddler and before I was born, so it was the only family home I had ever known. Everything felt familiar and warm, calming me a bit, even with H&H—as I lovingly, and also sometimes exasperatedly, referred to the twins—chanting at Grandma to let them taste the batter.

Dad took one look at me and said, "What's wrong, Blaire Bear?"

My dad and I have always had a special bond. Maybe it was because I was the baby of the family, maybe it was because I shared his deep love and appreciation for Holly Ridge and all of our town traditions, but regardless, I definitely do not relish having to be the one to share this news with him.

"Well, the whole town will know soon enough. I found out the reason my contract included such strong finish-the-project-or-else vibes."

Something in my tone alerted my mom that this wasn't going to be an easy conversation, so she turned to the twins. "I'll get these cookies into the oven. Why don't you two head into the living room and read for a few moments? When the cookies are done, we'll have some for dessert with lunch."

Though my niece and nephew were balls of energy, they also loved to read. The Greene bookworm gene was too strong to be stamped out by my brother-in-law's athletic prowess. They thundered into the next room, arguing over who was going to be able to read more pages before lunch was served.

Once Holland and Hollis were out of earshot, Dad turned to me.

"Okay, Blaire, what's going on?"

Dad did a good job of letting go of town duties and responsibilities once he retired and the council had taken over, trying to let the town move on while he transitioned to the next phase of his life. But I knew this wasn't going to be easy for him to hear.

"Well, the council has really made a mess of things. All of those projects the council undertook that were supposed to make money? Sure seems like they weren't at all successful and the town is bankrupt. If this year's Christmas festival isn't a success, Holly

Ridge is going to lose its town charter and get absorbed into Winterberry Glen."

I sat down roughly onto one of the kitchen stools with an audible huff, the magnitude of the situation I had just signed myself on to for the next nine months hitting me.

Dad leaned on the kitchen island, forcing me to look him in the eye. "I heard rumblings that things were bad, but I didn't realize they were this bad. Is that why they hired you?"

"Yes, though I don't have complete free rein. There's someone from Winterberry Glen who will be involved—keeping an eye on the planning and making sure things are fiscally responsible and all that."

I sat at the island in my parent's kitchen, surrounded by two of my biggest cheerleaders, all the comforting reminders of home and the scent of chocolate chip cookies wafting in the air, and yet I found myself too overwhelmed with the uncertainty of where to start first.

"Their CFO wasn't able to be at city hall with the council today for some reason, so I need to be in touch with him sometime this week to set up our first meeting, and then I'll find out more of what the oversight will look like. Until then, I think I'm just going to go upstairs and sleep for a few days. Hope that this is all just a bad dream."

My mom winced in sympathy, saying, "Well, at least wait another ten minutes, so you can sleep with your stomach full of warm chocolate chip cookies."

At this, my stomach growled, I don't even think I realized I was hungry, and the cookies did smell delicious.

Mom continued. "But I do wonder if you might feel better with at least doing a little bit of brainstorming about the festival? You've only been home for the last few days of the festival for the last several years, but I know you'll have ideas about how to freshen it up and make it exciting."

This was something that I loved about my family. They didn't sit here and make fake promises that everything would be okay, that I'd absolutely 100 percent succeed in this mountainous endeavor, but they did offer me supporting looks, chocolate chip cookies, and an idea that probably would, at the end of the day, make me feel better than a three-day nap. Though a three-hour nap after I made some lists and had some cookies wasn't totally out of the question. It was a trying morning, after all.

Chapter 2

Cole

Even as the Chief Financial Officer for Winterberry Glen, my view wasn't anything to write home about, but it was a space that was mine, and that's why I insisted Blaire join me here for our first meeting about the festival. I didn't want to spend more time in Holly Ridge than I had to. Plus, this way, she would know that I was in charge and wouldn't be easy to take advantage of, no matter how vulnerable she looked when she tucked her shiny brunette hair behind her ears when she was nervous.

Okay, fine, I may have spent some time researching Blaire Greene in preparation for this meeting. Chalk it up to curiosity about why the daughter of the last mayor Holly Ridge may ever have was the one they decided to bring in to oversee the festival in such an incredibly important year, but I needed to see who I was working with. I had learned over the years that I didn't deal well with surprises, and I found comfort in seeking as much information about who I would be working with as possible.

After just a few clips of her being interviewed by the local press and some image searches, it was obvious she loved the small-town life, and even worse, she loved Christmas. Why else would she dedicate her adult life to planning small-town festivals all over the tristate area? Honestly, she seemed to be quite competent and qualified for the job. Maybe no one would ever be qualified to run a festival that a town's existence depended on, but she definitely had experience in small-town festivals and a love for Holly Ridge, so she seemed as good a fit as any. I also noticed she favored blazers to project a powerful image to the press. Even when there was a hint of vulnerability in her eyes during one particularly tense interview alongside a government official named Mason, the blazer seemed to act as a suit of armor for Ms. Greene. I reminded myself I didn't care about Blaire, her fitness of any sort, or the future of Holly Ridge. That was why I had run the internet search, so I could get these mind-ramblings out of the way before we met in person.

Just then, I heard a knock on the door.

"Mr. Thomas?" Blaire asked from the doorway, looking around, uncertain if there should be a secretary or someone in the antechamber of my office to play watch dog.

"Ms. Greene," I responded, standing up to greet her. "Please come in."

I watched Blaire set her chin with her head held high and make her way into my office. *No vulnerability present this morning,* I thought, which was probably for the best. What was present were her piercing blue eyes, set beneath her long brunette hair, which rested in curls along the shoulders of her, *you guessed it,* blazer. This blazer didn't have the decency to be boxy, with chunky shoulder pads, but outlined her figure perfectly, giving her a feminine shape while keeping things professional. I didn't even know a blazer could do that. Suddenly, my mouth felt dry. I searched my desk for the water bottle I filled up every morning upon arrival at the office. I found it, right next to my monitor, as usual and unscrewed the lid, taking several generous swallows.

"How are you this morning, Mr. Thomas?" Blaire asked, settling into one of the chairs that were on the other side of my desk and shaking me out of my blazer-related thought soliloquy and subsequent case of Sahara-dry-mouth.

I sat down answering "Fine," placing the water bottle back on my desk. I was not interested in engaging in any small talk, just in getting Blaire the information she needed and getting her back out of my door, so I could get my focus back and get to work.

A flash of surprise flickered through Blaire's eyes at my curt response, but she pushed forward.

"I've been brainstorming since I met with the council last week about the scenario we find ourselves in, and I'm really excited to tell yo—"

"Before we start dreaming, let's go over these state-approved guidelines for my oversight of the project." I handed her the copy that I had waiting on my desk and watched as she took them in, her smile turning into more of a scowl with every line. Part of me wondered which she was going to address first—the fact that I had to give approval for every expenditure over $250, that we had to hold three town halls open to both communities over the course of the planning period, or the shortened timeline for the festival.

"The festival is only sixteen days long?" Blaire exclaimed.

The timeline it was, then.

"Why would you shorten it when it's more important than ever that it succeeds?" Blaire's cheeks were starting to redden as her indignation grew.

I assumed she wouldn't be pleased with the restrictions laid out for her as festival planner, but I hadn't expected how watching her reaction playing out on her body would have such an impact on mine, specifically in a tightening behind my zipper. *No,* I thought, trying to get my body back under control. Her passion and fury were *not* attractive, and in any case, we were *not* going there, not when my ticket out of Winterberry Glen was riding—*no pun intended!*—on the success of this project. The guidelines also clearly stated that a relationship between the two of us was forbidden to maintain ethical lines of approval.

"Yes, Ms. Greene," I responded evenly, not wanting to give away the turmoil I was feeling inside. "While the success of the festival is important to you and to Holly Ridge, we must consider the financial implications of the typical month-long festival. When the festival runs longer, it's more expensive to put on and the profit margin decreases. It's to your benefit to put your focus on a shorter period of time. If you do your job well, it will help your overall profit totals."

"*If* I do my job well?" Blaire stood at this point, our meeting clearly over now that she felt that I'd insulted her competence. "I've planned events for entities much larger than Holly Ridge and have always produced a healthy profit line. There's a reason I was hired to do this job."

"Oh, it's not because daddy put in a call?"

At this, Blaire's face was completely shuttered, devoid of any tells of emotions or that rosy hue I had found so alluring just a moment before. She was full-on ice queen.

"No, Mr. Thomas, *daddy* had nothing to do with my current position. Does your daddy have something to do with yours?"

It was my turn to shut down, even though I rationally realized that Blaire couldn't have any idea how deep her barb would strike. My dad had no idea I was still in Winterberry Glen, let alone have any hand in getting me the job I had today.

"Good day, Ms. Greene. Please be in touch with a loose schedule concept by the end of next week."

Blaire gathered up her notebook and bag, tucking her hair behind her ears and stalked to the door. With one last look over her shoulder, she said, "Bah humbug to you too, Mr. Thomas," and she swung out of the office door, letting it click shut behind her.

Chapter 3

Blaire

I was fuming as I walked out of the Winterberry Glen government building and strode to my car. What in the *world* gave Cole Thomas the right to assume I had been given this job because of who my father was? How did he even *know* who my father was in the first place? Glenians stayed out of Ridgeians business. Even if I wasn't quite sure what this feud was about, at least I understood that much.

Did he Google me? I thought as I opened the door to my blue SUV—something I was proud to say I had paid off six months ago. *Rookie mistake, Greene, always Google the opposition. Especially so you're not taken aback by their arresting brown eyes, their shiny, perfectly mussed-yet-professional brown hair, and shoulders so wide they should be carrying a yoke with pails of water on them, regardless of what century it was.*

Okay, so sue me. I had noticed that Cole Thomas was one good looking member of the naughty list, especially when you factored in those glasses that seemed to be my kryptonite, but I had to keep my eyes on the prize, and that prize was keeping Holly Ridge as its own town and throwing the best fucking Christmas festival New England had ever seen, even if it could only be two weeks long.

I felt I was now calm enough to at least drive the speed limit and not endanger everyone else on the road, so I started the car and pressed the speed dial to give Charlotte, my best friend since birth, a call. Charlotte had stayed in Holly Ridge after high school to help with her parents' bookstore and was one of the reasons I was so glad to be back home after being away for so long.

"So, how did it go?" she asked as soon as she answered the phone, not bothering with any greetings. Charlotte may have been on the receiving end of approximately forty-five anxiety texts a day over the past week, so she knew exactly why I was calling.

"Well, Char," I sighed, suddenly feeling way more hopeless than I had, now that my rage-fueled power walk was over, "I have to have any expenses over $250 approved, so essentially everything. They've cut the festival down to the last two weeks of December, and it feels like they're trying to set me up to fail."

"Oof," Charlotte responded, and I could picture her adorable button nose wrinkling as she took in my news, surrounded by books with her trusty Diet Coke can in her hand. "That doesn't sound like the best parameters for a massive financial success or a smooth and painless planning process. What was the Winterberry Glen official like?"

I snorted. "You mean, Mr. Stick-up-his-fine-ass, couldn't-pin-the-antlers-on-the-reindeer-if-he-had-his-eyes-open, one Mr. Cole Thomas? He's what you'd expect for a money guy who seems to hate Christmas. He insinuated I only got the job because of who my dad is."

I expected this to send Charlotte into a rage. She, more than anyone, knew how hard I had worked for all my opportunities, but she surprised me. "Wait, can we back up to the stick-up-his-*fine*-ass part? Is Mr. Heat Miser a certified hottie?"

Cursing myself for that slip, I knew there was no distracting her until I answered the question. "Mr. Thomas may not be exactly hard on the eyes, but he's the enemy here, so we're going to ignore any warm feelings I had when I looked at him for the first time and focus on the ice that gathered around my heart and anywhere else as soon as he opened his mouth."

Charlotte's eye roll could be heard through the phone. "Uh-huh. Okay, whatever you say, B. So, what's next?"

"Next up is me putting together a schedule outline for him to approve sometime next week. Luckily, I could vision board a Christmas festival in my sugarplum-filled dreams, but I've never had to work with such a short timeline before. Some things are going to have to get cut." I sighed heavily, wondering what portions of Christmas joy were going to end up left out of the festival this year.

"Well, I know you, and I know that having a goal and a plan is the best possible thing you can do, so why don't you go home and get the binder I know you started already and bring it over to the store? We can brainstorm how to fit in all the town traditions and the new and innovative stuff I know you're dying to get into the schedule? There's story time this morning, so the store will be swamped with wee ones and exhausted parents, but I'll be sure to save your favorite armchair for you, and we can work it out."

As usual, Charlotte came through with helping me take my mile-a-minute thoughts and help me focus on what I needed to do next.

"That sounds perfect, Char. Thanks so much. I'll see you soon. Oh, and be sure to hold a copy of that new fantasy romance that came out earlier this week. I feel like I'm going to need an escape here *realllly* soon," I responded, swinging my car into my parents' drive, my Head-Bitch-In-Charge energy restored and ready to tackle the parameter list Cole and I had been given and map out a bitchin' festival.

I exited the car, so focused on running up to my room and grabbing the exact binder Charlotte had referenced—the cascading tabs were just gorgeous, by the way—that I didn't notice my sister walking down the sidewalk to climb into her hybrid Lexus SUV until I almost ran straight into her.

"Whoa there, Blaire. Watch where you're going!" Gretchen exclaimed, grabbing onto my arm to stop me from toppling off the sidewalk. "I guess the meeting went well if you're in such a hurry to get to your binder and get started on the next steps?"

"How did you know I had a meeting this morning? Wait, why are you here in the middle of the day? Are the twins okay?" I asked.

Gretchen's perfectly lined light pink lips twitched. She hated when I answered a question with a question, something I did around her because I get nervous when she puts on her cross-examination voice.

Gretchen had never actively done anything to make me feel inferior, but our relationship was a strained one. Since she was ten years older than me, she was always the example I was measuring myself against. Her pretty blond hair made me hate my perfectly fine brown hair. Her Juris Doctor from an Ivy League school made my project management degree from a state school seem like nothing to write home about. Her career advancement in private firms created the urge in me to always move on to bigger and better festivals. And let's not even get started on the beautiful husband and cookie-cutter twins—a perfect family all secured and created, while anyone I managed to date either undermined my successes or belittled my accomplishments in front of others.

All these comparisons were internal. I knew my parents were proud of me, and I knew Gretchen loved me, but I honestly felt like all the parts of Blaire would always be less than even a portion of the parts of Gretchen.

"The twins are fine," Gretchen responded. "Hollis forgot his inhaler, so I dropped an extra one by on my lunch break. Mom mentioned you should be on your way back from your meeting with the Winterberry Glen CFO soon. So again, how did it go?"

"There will be some bumps in the road as Cole and I figure out how to work together, but I think it will all be okay," I said, glossing over how I really felt, like I usually did when I talked to her. She had real problems, like a sixty-hour work week, an asthmatic son, and who knows what else to worry about. She didn't want to hear me talk about the festival she's barely had time for since she turned sixteen.

"I'm headed to grab my binder now,"—*honestly, was I that predictable?*—"and am going to meet Charlotte at the store to talk through some roadblocks."

"Sounds like a great way to spend the afternoon," Gretchen replied. "Be sure to tell Charlotte and her parents I said hi and let me know if I can help brainstorm anything with you, too. I know the festival hasn't been *my thing* in the past, but we stayed in Holly Ridge to raise the kids because we wanted them to experience small-town life. I'd love to do my part to help save it."

As I watched her get in her car and drive away, I couldn't help but wonder now that I was home again and older if my relationship with Gretchen would change. I definitely had some mindsets of my own to challenge when it came to my internal comparisons, but I was seeing a new silver-lining to my homecoming that hadn't been there before.

Cole

You don't become the Chief Financial Officer of your hometown by age thirty by accident. Honestly, nothing in my life happened by accident if I could help it. So many things in my early life had been outside of my control. I didn't pick that I was born in Winterberry Glen to two parents who were better off apart than they were together. I didn't choose to live in a town that held the short-stick of an inter-town feud. I didn't choose to have the enjoyment of Christmas taken from me at the age of ten.

Given all that, it might surprise many people to find I still lived in the town I was born in. Well, that was a choice. I chose to go to the state university thirty miles away to stay close to my mom, who didn't seem to agree she was better off without my dad. I majored in business and governance because numbers and facts were something that had always made sense to me. I embraced the job offer in the Winterberry Glen CFO's office after I completed an internship the summer before my senior year, because it provided me with security as I finished out my college days and allowed me to continue to look after Mom. I worked nights and weekends for the old CFO, so the City Council had no choice but to hire me for the job when old Berry White retired two years ago.

I was at my desk looking over last month's audit reports when my cell phone buzzed. Glancing at the screen, I saw my best friend's name on the caller ID, and noting the time, knew exactly why he was calling.

"Hi Austin, I'm not late for dinner yet, because our reservation is still thirty minutes away," I said in lieu of a greeting.

Austin's sigh reached my ears loud and clear over the line. "You're the only person in the Glen who thinks we need a reservation to hit up Muggsies on a weeknight, but this is my 'thirty-minute warning, Cole. Put down the paperwork and come join the people' call. I'd prefer to not be stood up again."

I winced. His comment was accurate. I had the tendency to get lost in numbers and spreadsheets and forget about bodily needs such as eating, sometimes at the cost of my friend's patience and goodwill. Even when someone has been your best friend for almost two decades, it's still nice to show up to dinner on time occasionally.

"Got it, bud. Your thoughtfulness and care are appreciated. I'm on my last spreadsheet. I'll see you in thirty."

As I hung up the phone, my eye caught on the picture of me and Austin that I kept next to the photo of me and my mom on my desk. The photo of with Austin was from a baseball game we went to last summer. Austin had on his signature flannel shirt as usual, sunglasses tucked into the pocket, his dark blond hair in its usual disarray, and his hazel eyes seemed to smile at everyone he greeted. Austin was just a happy, handsome guy. I was almost his opposite, standing next to him wearing a team shirt, my dark hair locked into place, with a smile on my face that didn't quite seem to reach the brown eyes behind my square glasses. It's not that I wasn't happy to be at the game and spending time with my best friend. My eyes just didn't light up on command the way his seemed to.

Glancing outside the window to the left of my desk, I was somewhat surprised to see that the sun had set, but it wasn't unusual for me to leave the office after dark, especially in the days when the sun set before 5:00 p.m. I had gotten through everything I wanted to after my morning meeting with Blaire Greene, Holly Ridge golden child and potential savior of their Christmas festival.

The sooner this project was over, the better, not only so I could distance myself from the relationship between Winterberry Glen and Holly Ridge, but also physically distance myself from Winterberry Glen as well. The state audit office let me know that if everything with this situation went smoothly, regardless of the outcome—the state didn't care if the towns were separate or together, they just wanted balanced budgets—there would be a job waiting for me in the state's audit office operations. While my reasons for staying in Winterberry Glen for as long as I had weren't ones I regretted, I was feeling like it was time to move on and move my life out of the stalemate it had been in for years. Was working for the state audit office and moving to the state capital my dream? I don't even think I could tell you what my dream job was, but it would move me out of this town and all the terrible memories that went along with it and that would be worth it.

The only thing the state audit office was ultra-specific I had to do during the Holly Ridge oversight process was avoid any sort of personal relationship with Blaire Greene. I wasn't going to let those blazers Blaire seemed to favor get in the way of my focus and concentration toward this opportunity, no matter how good her shiny brunette hair smelled from across my desk.

Besides, avoiding a personal relationship with Blaire wouldn't be hard—you could ask Austin over a beer at Muggsies. He'd be glad to spill all of my secrets—I avoided all emotional connections when it came to relationships. I saw what marriage and commitment could turn into at the hands of my parents, and worse, I saw what losing even a toxic marriage could do to a person. I didn't want to repeat that pattern any more than I wanted to stay in this town I grew up in.

Speaking of Austin, even with his thirty-minute warning, if I didn't move now, I was definitely going to be late. I stood up from my desk, made sure that any papers that I hadn't filed away throughout the course of the day were stacked neatly and spaced evenly along the surface of my desk. I grabbed my jacket from the coat tree just inside my office door, turned off the lights, and headed down the stairwell to the side entrance that hit the sidewalk in front of the Winterberry Glen government building. As I walked the two blocks to dinner, I took in Main Street. While it didn't spark any warm fuzzies inside my hardened heart, I also couldn't exactly see any major flaws that would lead to Holly Ridge feeling that their downtown was so much better. Sure, we had more of a main street vibe than a town-square-built-around-a-gazebo energy, but it still seemed to have the potential to be charming, if you got off on that sort of thing.

Not a minute too soon—*these March evenings could be brisk* —I opened the door to Muggsies and was greeted with a rush of warm air and the familiar sounds of my favorite brew pub. I nodded to Angela, the hostess on duty this evening, saying, "Is Austin already back at our booth?"

Angela smiled and nodded in the affirmative.

Even though Austin gave me a hard time about my reservations, it wasn't because I was worried we wouldn't get a table. It's because I wanted my favorite table, the booth in the back corner. Being CFO of a small town where everyone knew your everyone, even when you weren't employed by the town government, came with its . . . . challenges, and since the Holly Ridge news had dropped last week, I anticipated there might be more interest than usual in grabbing my ear for a few minutes. Our back corner booth, at least, mostly eliminated pass-by traffic, and by sitting with my back to the wall, I could see anyone approaching us.

Austin was in the booth as Angela promised, and he had a beer waiting for me as well. I slid into the booth, picked up the draft, and cheersed him saying, "This is why I pick up your thirty-minute warning calls. Thanks for ordering ahead."

"I figured tonight might be a two-beer event," Austin replied, acknowledging how well he knew my moods and habits. "I assumed it wouldn't be the worst thing to have a beer waiting for you, so you could still be home and tucked in by nine."

I chuckled at my best friend, whose regular in-person presence would be one thing I would miss most about the Glen when I moved on next year.

"And why would tonight be a two-beer event?" I asked, not bothering to correct him, but I wanted to be sure I knew what was on his mind, so I wasn't tricked into revealing too much of myself for a casual Wednesday evening.

"Because you had to meet with someone from Holly Ridge today, and regularly for the next nine months, *and* those conversations will center on the Christmas festival," Austin replied evenly.

I nodded in acknowledgment and took another sip of my beer.

"And your brunette weakness is definitely going to kick in over a certain Ms. Greene," he added nonchalantly.

I suspected he had waited intentionally until I was mid-sip to drop that observation into conversation. Choking slightly before swallowing, I asked, "What is that supposed to mean?"

"C'mon, Cole. I know brunette is your type, and from what my date last night said, she was voted "Most Likely to Succeed" in high school, so I'm sure her competence is going to only make her more attractive to you."

Austin didn't observe the feud when it came to his dating pool. Any interested girl or guy on either side of the river was fair game for him. This created some scandal among the older crowd of our fellow townsfolk. No, not that he was dating around, or dated on all ends of the gender spectrum, but because sometimes his dates were from Holly Ridge and Austin was born and raised right here in Winterberry Glen. These towns may be progressive in many ways, but dating someone from across the river? Now that's just not done, according to many of the over-fifty crowd.

"She may have hair coloring that I sometimes find myself preferring on a woman," I hedged, "but she's from Holly Ridge, and we're going to be talking Christmas and the festival for nine months straight, which is a boner killer if I've ever heard one. And anyway, the state audit office explicitly outlined that any personal relationship between myself and Blaire was completely off-limits." I realized I was somehow at the bottom of my beer, and we hadn't even ordered food yet.

"Besides, I may have insinuated that her dad was the only reason she got the job in the first place, so even if I was at all interested in a personal relationship—which we know I'm not, because falling in love makes a fool out of people and I refuse to be a fool —she definitely wouldn't even be remotely interested."

Austin grinned at me over his pint glass. "Thee doth protest too much, methinks."

"I think thee might be an idiot." Not my best comeback, but the beer and no dinner was getting to me.

"Can we drop this now and eat before everyone realizes I'm hiding back here and they ask me even more questions than you have about Blaire and the festival planning process?"

"Oh man, she's forbidden and you're already protesting this much after just one meeting? You're done for," Austin replied with glee in his eyes.

But to his credit, he did move the evening along with his next breath. "When I ordered these beers, I put in for potato skins for me and the hummus platter for you. I'm sure they'll be here any second."

From there, our evening progressed as our dinners normally

do, catching up on Austin's most recent dating escapades, work, and whatever sport happened to be in season. The conversation never turned back to Blaire officially, and I'd deny it if I was ever asked, but I did find myself spending the rest of the evening trying to convince myself I didn't need to go back to my office to grab my Blaire file to go over once more before bed.

Chapter 3.5

To: CThomas@winterberryglen.gov
From: BGreene@hollyridge.gov
Date: March 17, 2:45 p.m.
Subject: Holiday Festival Schedule Draft

Dear Mr. Thomas,

As requested, here is a draft of the holiday festival schedule for you to review. I've included attachments outlining budgets for each of the events, appearances, and performances. I organized the schedule in several ways; one version by date and time, one version by location, and one version by target demographics.

Also attached is a marketing plan and timeline, which you'll note starts with the announcement of the dates of the festival on April 1st, so I hope we can move quickly on approval. If you have any questions or would like to meet in person to go over anything here, please let me know. My schedule is flexible right now!

Best wishes,
Blaire Greene
Holly Ridge Festival Planner

To: BGreene@hollyridge.gov
From: CThomas@winterberryglen.gov
Date: March 17, 3:07 p.m.
Subject: Re: Holiday Festival Schedule Draft

Dear Ms. Greene,

Now that my retinas have recovered from all the colors you used on your various spreadsheets, I can see that your budget exceeds the amount allotted to you in the agreement by $10,000. Please adjust your schedule and budget accordingly to bring it under budget.

Warmest regards,
Cole Thomas
Winterberry Glen CFO

To: CThomas@winterberryglen.gov
From: BGreene@hollyridge.gov
Date: March 17, 3:15 p.m.
Subject: Re: Re: Holiday Festival Schedule Draft

Dear Mr. Thomas,

I apologize for injecting a bit of color and brightness into your life with my charts and schedules. I will be sure to adequately warn

you next time that some of us work in more than just black and
red inked spreadsheets all day.

I do hope that you were able to note that while the budget was
$10,000 over what was allotted to Holly Ridge in the agreement,
that I was planning to bring in $20,000 more in sponsorships
than the original budgets estimated, giving the budget cushion for
unexpected overages and drops in anticipated sponsor dollars.
Certainly, given that kind of projection, the budget can move
forward as anticipated and attached?

Best wishes,
Blaire Greene
Holly Ridge Festival Planner

To: BGreene@hollyridge.gov
From: CThomas@winterberryglen.gov
Date: March 17, 11:15 p.m.
Subject: Re: Re: Re: Holiday Festival Schedule Draft

Dear Ms. Greene,

I believe that the International Space Station could also use a
warning before you print off another copy of your schedule. They
will want to be prepared to explain the bright phenomenon origi-
nating from your small town.

Work within the approved budget until sponsorships are signed
and agreed to. As those agreements come in, you can increase the
budget and adjust the festival schedule accordingly. Your City
Council has made too many promises it couldn't deliver on for
the state to budge on this point. We must see the money before
you are able to spend it.

Warmest regards,
Cole Thomas
Winterberry Glen CFO

To: CThomas@winterberryglen.gov
From: BGreene@hollyridge.gov
Date: April 1, 10:07 a.m.
Subject: April Fools?

Dear Mr. Thomas,

Thank you ever so much for putting in the effort to send me a letter posing as Taylor Swift turning down my invitation to perform at the festival. That was a trap you fell right into. I felt you had stopped listening during our last meeting, so I was testing you to see if you were paying attention. And, I'll have you know, Taylor and I *would* be best friends if we ever met, and I think I have a wonderful voice.

Best wishes,
Blaire Greene
Holly Ridge Festival Planner

P.S. Not an April Fool's joke: please see the report I attached on the origins of the Holly Ridge/Winterberry Glen feud from my research at the Holly Ridge library. My feelings will be greatly hurt if you don't give me your thoughts when we meet next.

To: BGreene@hollyridge.gov
From: CThomas@winterberryglen.gov
Date: April 2, 11:06 a.m.
Subject: Re: April Fools?

Dear Ms. Greene,

I regret to admit I know this now, after only a few short weeks of knowing you, but you've taught me that Taylor does love her cats. Since you sing like one, I suppose I must admit you're correct that you would be best friends.

Please don't make me read this report. I'll have Diet Coke in the fridge for you from now on at our meetings if you don't.

Warmest Regards,
Cole Thomas
Winterberry Glen CFO

To: CThomas@winterberryglen.gov
From: BGreene@hollyridge.gov
Date: April 2, 4:05 p.m.
Subject: Re: Re: April Fools?

Dear Mr. Thomas,

You have found my weakness: a fridge full of Diet Coke. You have yourself a deal, but can you also put in a good word for me with the Winterberry Glen librarian? I want to see how your records differ from ours, and she won't take my calls.

See you tomorrow.

Best wishes,
Blaire Green
Holly Ridge Festival Planner

Chapter 4

May

    Blaire

Well, it finally arrived. The first of three town halls I had to host with Cole about the festival. We were holding two—this one and the final one right before Thanksgiving—here in Holly Ridge, and the second one was going to be held in Winterberry Glen. I guess because they had financial oversight the state thought they should host a town hall as well. We were gathered in the Holly Ridge community center, which would serve as the home for the gingerbread house decorating contest display and emergency center for the festival. The recessed lighting bore down harshly on the room, the same lighting had illuminated my dad during the many town hall meetings he oversaw when I was growing up. I took a deep breath, organized the papers in front of me one more time and prepared myself for the meeting to begin.

As I looked out at the audience. Seats were filling faster than I had anticipated. I saw that people were naturally dividing themselves—Holly Ridge on the left and Winterberry Glen on the right.

Oh boy, I thought to myself, *this has the potential to get way out of control*.

This was the closest I had ever been to Cole. Usually separated by that monstrosity of a desk he used in his office when we met once a week for the past two months, and I couldn't help but notice he smelled good. Clean laundry, a pinch of cinnamon, and something else I couldn't quite place without leaning closer and taking a big whiff, and nope, I was not letting that happen. I was still fuming over his latest dig at my spreadsheets: "At least I'll be able to line my mom's litter box for the next several months with old versions of this schedule." Urgh. Our organizational/planning styles did not mesh up at all. After all of our meetings, I did know that much, but I also felt that I was growing on him, like his grumpiness was starting to grow on me. Collegially, that is.

Cole glanced my way.

"It's 6:59, we should start right on time."

I honestly agreed with him, but just to be a bit contrary, I said, "We'll give people a few minutes to file in. I saw a long line inside Jitters when I was walking through the square to get to the community center."

Cole's jaw tensed at my dissent from his plan, but as we were on my turf, he didn't push any further. I bit my lip to keep from smiling at the win, no matter how small, and reviewed the detailed agenda I had made myself one more time, even though I could probably recite it from memory. Out of the corner of my eye, I saw Cole bend to retrieve something from his tan messenger bag. *Ah, cinnamon gum, that explained part of his alluring scent.*

At 7:05 on the dot, nodding at Cole, I raised my voice to quiet the crowd.

"Hi everyone, and welcome to the first of three meetings about the Holly Ridge Christmas Festival! For anyone who doesn't know me, I'm Blaire Greene, the festival planner for this year. I grew up in Holly Ridge and the festival holds some of my favorite memories and I really think this year's festival has the potential to be the best one yet, even with the massive stakes involved. Cole, do you want to take a minute to introduce yourself?"

"Good evening, I'm Cole Thomas, Winterberry Glen, CFO."

I waited for a beat. Then I realized that was indeed all Cole was going to offer as his introduction, so I stuck a smile on my face and carried on.

"All right, then . . . let's get started! I thought we could start tonight by—"

"How much money exactly does this festival have to bring in for the state audit office to allow Holly Ridge to remain its own entity?" a tall, bald man on the Winterberry Glen side asked, while scraping his chair across the tile.

"Those numbers aren't public information at this point in time, and it's a bit in flux based on a number of factors, including the results from the last census. We'll have a question-and-answer portion at—"

"Yeah, buddy, save your questions for the question-and-answer portion!" Earl, from the Holly Ridge repair shop, growled angrily across the aisle.

"You know, you interrupted her, too," Cole drily observed from next to me. "Why don't we let Ms. Greene lay out her agenda for the evening, and we'll go from there?"

Annoyed and yet slightly grateful that Cole had spoken up for me, I took a deep breath and started again.

"Like I was saying, I thought we would start tonight by going over the bare bones of the festival, like the dates and some of the major events—"

"I saw the festival is going to be sixteen days long," said a businesswoman from the Winterberry Glen side, who looked like she came straight from work at a bank or law firm. "Doesn't that seem to be a bit too long, considering the potentially serious implications on financial resources that Winterberry Glen will have to absorb, if and when the festival fails at its goal?"

I braced myself, knowing the Ridge residents weren't going to let that one go unanswered.

"Sixteen days is *too long*?" Ethel from Ethel's Pies and Potpourri exclaimed, her tuft of white hair just visible in the back of the Holly Ridge crowd. "This festival has run from Thanksgiving to Christmas for as long as I've been a Holly Ridge resident, and the fact that they're shortening it to just over two weeks is absolutely criminal!"

"Criminal? Your city councillors are the criminals. That's why we may have to swoop in and clean up your mess!" the first interrupting man interjected. "I think the state audit office is being too lenient even letting you *have* a festival this year."

At this, the room erupted into bedlam as both sides hurled insults at the other. Alison, the newborn baby belonging to Lydia, the owner of the Holly Ridge dance studio, woke up at the noise and added her cries to the fold, while a service dog belonging to one of Winterberry Glen's residents started barking, apparently trying to warn her owner that their blood pressure was getting too high. I sat in absolute shock. I guess I had never been in a room with this many residents of both towns at once, especially to discuss an issue which could so greatly impact the future of the area.

A piercing whistle entered the fray from my right, and I looked over to see Cole standing on his chair, his fingers to his lips.

Why is that power move so attractive? Should I practice it when I get home? I briefly thought before Cole's booming voice snapped me out of it.

"That is enough!" Cole thundered. "We will upload the handouts from tonight's meeting to both town portals by 10:00 a.m. tomorrow. This town hall is canceled, and I highly suggest you do not plan to attend any of the future meetings on this topic unless you can plan to do so quietly and respectfully."

The shocked members of both towns blinked up at Cole and then slowly gathered their things. I looked toward the back of the room and noticed members of both towns' Sheriff's offices standing by the doorway. Apparently, the noise had drawn some attention to the scanner waves. All the attendees filed out of the room, grumbling, and shooting dirty looks at each other, but luckily, keeping all hands, legs, and walking sticks to themselves as they exited.

I sat in a stunned silence and jumped to feel a hand on my shoulder.

"Are you okay?" Cole asked, looking down at me from his towering height. I nodded slowly, not sure how to answer that question yet. I'd never had a meeting go so off the rails so quickly, and town halls were known for their quirky outbursts. He opened his mouth like he wanted to say more, but just as quickly shut it, swung his messenger bag over his head, turned, and briskly walked out of the room without looking back.

Chapter 5

Cole

I'll admit it, I didn't feel great about leaving Blaire behind in the community center with that shocked look on her face, but I wasn't great with emotions. Blaire wore her emotions on her sleeve, whether it was about her spreadsheets and schedules, about the hometown she so obviously loved to her core, or about whatever Taylor Swift album she had been listening to on her drive over for our weekly meetings inspired in her.

I sat in my car in the community center parking lot, trying to determine my next move, when I saw Blaire making her way to her car in the same lot. Her shoulders slumped in a defeated posture, like she had the weight of the world on them, as she fumbled to find her keys. Making my mind up on the spot, I jumped out of the driver's seat, calling, "Hey, Greene, want to grab a drink at Pepper's?"

I saw Blaire give a start, and I winced realizing I had startled her. Keeping my eyes on her face, I watched her bite her lip as she weighed my offer like the keys she had successfully freed from the depths of her bag. "Sounds good, Thomas. I'll see you there."

Blaire opened the door to her SUV and climbed inside. I tried not to let my eyes linger too long on her legs as they folded in after the rest of her, and blew out a long breath, wondering if this was a bad idea.

At least we were meeting at Pepper's, the chain restaurant that shared the Wally World parking lot on the towns' borders. No one from either town often frequented the location, preferring to eat at the local restaurants within their own town limits. This left Pepper's to serve customers from surrounding towns who came to take advantage of the big box store's deals. This meant we wouldn't be bothered by anyone who was at the meeting or had heard about how it all turned out and wanted to get in their two cents.

Pulling into the parking lot at Pepper's, I parked next to Blaire's SUV—*you couldn't miss it with that bright blue color*—and met her on the sidewalk. We walked together into the restaurant lobby in silence and greeted by a hostess named Nancy.

"Hi there! Welcome to Pepper's! How many for you this evening?"

We both looked at each other.

"Just two," Blaire answered. "Maybe a booth in the corner?"

"Oh, secluded!" Nancy winked, grabbing rolled silverware and napkins from the hostess stand and turning around. "Follow me!"

I gestured for Blaire to walk in front of me, and followed her back to the corner booth, which I couldn't help but notice was, in fact, incredibly secluded. It was an extra good thing no one would see us here. The last thing we needed was any hints of impropriety between us, especially considering the conditions the state audit office had put down on the terms of us working together and my offer.

"Enjoy!" Nancy said joyfully before spinning off to head back to the hostess stand.

I glanced across the table to see Blaire studiously examining the menu.

"Hungry?" I asked her.

Blaire's cheeks reddened, and she immediately put the menu back on the table.

"Not really. I just picked up the menu out of habit."

Before I could comment, Nancy stepped back up to the table, bringing with her two glasses of ice water and straws.

"Guess I'm playing double duty tonight. I'll be serving y'all as well. Can I get you started with something to drink?"

"Sauvignon Blanc, please," Blaire replied, handing her menu over and then immediately grabbing one of the straws Nancy had put on the table, continuing to keep her hands busy and her eyes away from mine.

"I'll have a draft beer please, an IPA, whatever you have on tap," handing my menu over too, deciding to follow Blaire's lead on not ordering any food, keeping things just to the drink she had agreed to. That way, either of us could make a quick escape, though I was surprised to find I didn't want to be anywhere else at this moment.

"I'll have those right out," Nancy smiled, bounding over to the serving station to put in our orders before heading to the bar to shoot the breeze with the bartender.

"So," I started, "that meeting was really something, wasn't it?"

Blaire snorted out a laugh before burying her face in her hands. "Oh my goodness, it was a total fucking disaster," she groaned before lifting her face to meet my eyes. "I had imagined a million different ways that town hall could have gone. A lot of them were negative, but none of them were *that* bad. I thought we were going to have a full-out brawl on our hands before you stepped in and silenced them." She swallowed. "Thanks for that, by the way . . . you know, for taking charge and cutting them off before it got even more out of hand."

It was my turn to avoid her eyes. I took a long sip of water before responding.

"It was nothing. I didn't want to be liable if Mrs. Krazinsky had a heart attack right there in the community center and she was transported to the county hospital by Holly Ridge EMS services. I never would have heard the end of it."

Something flickered across Blaire's face as she digested my response. But before I had a chance to investigate any further, Nancy was back with our drinks. "One glass of wine, one IPA, both nice and cold for you kids!" Nancy sing-songed. "Just flag me down if you need another round or decide you want to put in a food order."

Blaire and I both took several quick swallows of our drinks as Nancy walked away.

"What if we did the next two town halls as virtual webinars?" I suggested. "We could host the next one on the Winterberry Glen account and the final on Holly Ridge's account, so it still fulfills the hosting terms laid out from the beginning, but then we have some control and moderation over the questions and outbursts?"

I watched as Blaire considered this.

"That's actually a pretty good idea," Blaire admitted. "If this was pre-pandemic, I would be worried about access and user knowledge, but everyone knows how to video conference at this point, plus we won't have to worry about muting and unmuting if it's webinar style."

"Okay, great." I responded, ignoring the warmth in my chest at Blaire saying I had a good idea. That had to be the IPA setting in.

"I'll get one of our summer interns set up for moderating the Q&A section for the next town hall since that's ours to host, and we can circle back on how that goes before you host again this fall."

"Sounds good," Blaire affirmed, tucking her long, brown hair behind her ear.

"So, with that out of the way, can I ask you something? You don't have to answer if you don't want to, but I can't say I haven't wondered a lot over the past few months. It's clear you hate Holly Ridge and the festival, which isn't that unusual for someone from Winterberry Glen, but what is unusual is that I don't get a ton of hometown pride from you. Why are you still in this area, working for the town, if you don't love it here?"

I can't say I was surprised that Blaire managed to suss this out about me. She was far too observant for my comfort level. What did surprise me was that she felt comfortable asking me. I thought it was clear I preferred to shut down personal conversations. She must have been feeling her own warmth from her almost empty glass of wine. What surprised me even more was that I wanted to give her some sort of answer.

I spoke slowly, trying to decide how much of myself to give away to this woman.

"My mom still lives in town. I've always thought that numbers made sense, and I interned with the Winterberry Glen government in college. When a job opened up the summer after I graduated, it . . . made sense to stay."

Blaire nodded, processing and seeming to accept this explanation as all she would likely get on that for now.

"Okay, and then the festival oversight? What made you agree to take that on when the state audit office called?"

"Well," I responded, "it's not like I had much choice in the matter when they called."

I wasn't sure I wanted Blaire to know about the job offer. Why? I wasn't sure about that either. But before I had too long to think about it, I was saved by Nancy.

"Another round for you kids tonight?" Nancy asked, stopping by with her tray propped on her hip.

Blaire and I made eye contact, and I shook my head no. Blaire nodded her head in agreement and said, "Just the checks, please!"

Nancy smiled.

"Sure thing, one check?"

"Separate checks," Blaire and I both responded in unison. I didn't appreciate the knowing smile on Nancy's face as she nodded and walked away to prep our checks.

Blaire spun her empty wineglass by the stem.

"You know, I think the biggest reason I wanted tonight to go well is I wanted my family to know it went well. My sister leads these high-pressure depositions all the time and my dad oversaw dozens of town halls in that very room, and I've never heard them talk about a situation that got out of hand quite like this."

I wasn't sure how to respond to that. This was the first time Blaire had revealed her insecurities when it came to her seemingly perfect family, but then again, our time together was more often spent arguing about expenses or schedules, not really being transparent with each other.

"Here you go, kids," Nancy said as she returned with our separate checks, her impeccable timing on display again. "Y'all have a great night and I hope to see you back at Pepper's soon!"

Blaire shook her head and smiled at Nancy, taking the pen out of the receipt holder and signing her name after adding a generous tip. I guess that was the end of the emotional honesty portion of the evening for both of us. After we closed out our bills, Blaire and I walked back toward our cars.

"I hope you're feeling a bit better about the town hall meeting," I said as we approached Blaire's car. "I'll post the documents on our portal when I get home, and hopefully the webinar approach will help the next two meetings be a bit more productive."

Blaire nodded. "I'll post the documents to Holly Ridge's portal tonight, too. We'll see if I can keep off the Holly Ridge community online group tonight. I don't think I want to see what their reactions are."

A piece of Blaire's hair fell into her face, and she just looked so defeated again, which was the opposite of how I wanted her to feel after my reassurance and our drinks.

I reached toward that wayward lock of hair and tucked it behind Blaire's ear. Her eyes shot up to mine and then flickered toward my mouth. I couldn't let myself go there, so I released Blaire's hair and reached behind her to open her driver's side door. Blaire didn't move out of my way as I expected her to, and my nose ended up brushing her hair, right where I had replaced that stray strand, inhaling her honey scent.

Blaire was boxed in between her open door and my body. My body refused to move when my face was inches from hers. My eyes strayed to her lips, her tongue peaked out of her mouth to wet them, and I found I wanted to taste those lips, have my tongue tangled with hers.

Suddenly an alarm sounded in the Wally World parking lot across the way, and just like that, the spell was broken. I remembered exactly whose scent was intoxicating me. Getting involved with Blaire would void my ticket out of Winterberry Glen. Also, there was the minor fact that we couldn't stand each other, and even if that changed, Blaire was the sort of girl one would form a real attachment to. An attachment I never intended to form with anyone. I felt myself taking a sudden step back.

"I'm . . . I'm sorry," I stammered, and turning away from Blaire, I rushed to my car. For the second time in one night, I was leaving Blaire with a shocked look on her face, but it was clear I needed to get home. Trying to get closer to her would obviously lead to my own destruction.

Chapter 5.5

To: BGreene@hollyridge.gov
From: CThomas@winterberryglen.gov
Date: May 20, 2:45 p.m.
Subject: Virtual Meeting Calendar Invite

Dear Ms. Greene,

Please see the recurring meeting invite using Winterberry Glen's video conferencing software. Going forward, we will meet virtually for our weekly check-in meetings.

Warmest Regards,
Cole Thomas
Winterberry Glen CFO

To: CThomas@winterberryglen.gov
From: BGreene@hollyridge.gov
Date: May 21, 8:07 a.m.
Subject: Re: Virtual Meeting Calendar Invite

Dear Mr. Thomas,

Invitation received, but can you please clarify why we're moving to virtual check-ins? While you refuse to come to my favorite coffee shop in Holly Ridge to make our meetings more comfortable, and it'll be a relief to not have to worry about spilling too many pens across your desk and annoy you, I do think face to face can be more effective. I can say I'd be reluctantly happy to continue coming to the government center to continue our meetings. I'll stop suggesting other locations.

Best wishes,
Blaire Greene
Holly Ridge Festival Planner

To: BGreene@hollyridge.gov
From: CThomas@winterberryglen.gov
Date: May 21, 9:16 a.m.
Subject: Re: Re: Virtual Meeting Calendar Invite

Dear Ms. Greene,

I think it's best we meet virtually. It will save you time on commuting and give you more time for blazer shopping. If it's good enough for the town halls, we should lead by example and meet that way as well.

Warmest regards,
Cole Thomas
Winterberry Glen CFO

To: CThomas@winterberryglen.gov
From: BGreene@hollyridge.gov
Date: May 21, 11:56 a.m.
Subject: Re: Re: Re: Virtual Meeting Calendar Invite

Dear Mr. Thomas,
Is this because of the Pepper's parking lot? Seriously? Are we 13? I'm going to make the most obnoxious video background I can, and you can't stop me. All the colors. And just wait until we get to my screen shares. Ready your retinas, Thomas.

Best wishes,
Blaire Greene
Holly Ridge Festival Planner

To: BGreene@hollyridge.gov
From: CThomas@winterberryglen.gov
Date: May 22, 4:03 p.m.
Subject: Re: Re: Re: Re: Virtual Meeting Calendar Invite

Dear Ms. Greene,

I'm certain I don't know to what you are referring, especially not on this government e-mail channel.

See you virtually tomorrow.

Warmest regards,
Cole Thomas
Winterberry Glen CFO

Austin (8:05 p.m.): Dude, are you okay? I just saw you running and it looked like you had been at it for a while, but we worked out this morning.

Austin (8:06 p.m.): I also heard that a certain brunette wasn't seen at the government center for your weekly meeting today. Could that possibly be the motivation for the double workout?

Cole (8:46 p.m.): This town has a gossip problem, and it always seems to involve you. Ms. Greene and I met today.

Austin (8:53 p.m.): Uh-oh, back to Ms. Greene? What'd you do, sneak her in the back door?

Cole (8:55 p.m.): It's a government center, not a college residence hall. I don't sneak anyone anywhere. We decided to meet virtually for the foreseeable future.

Austin (8:56 p.m.): Is that a real we or a royal we?

Cole (9:03 p.m.): Okay, maybe I decreed and didn't leave much room for refusal. But after what almost happened in the Pepper's parking lot the other night, we need some space from each other.

Austin (9:05 p.m.): Pepper's? Parking lot? Space? You're being very cryptic, Cole. Don't make me call up my BFF Nancy. I know she'll give me the surveillance tapes.

Cole (9:07 p.m.): I've said too much.

Austin (9:10 p.m.): Nope, not even close to enough. The agenda for this week's dinner just got rearranged. For once, I will not be the first topic of conversation. Thank goodness, it's exhausting being the center of attention. Maybe I'll print one out. Make it color coded. That seems to get under your skin just the right amount.

Cole (9:15 p.m.): I hate you. See you tomorrow.

Austin (9:17 p.m.): *cat-paw-waving.gif*

Charlotte (11:05 p.m.): Okay, I'm finally done with homework after the author event at the store today, and I'm cashing in on my reward.

Charlotte (11:05 p.m.): How was the virtual meeting?

Charlotte (11:06 p.m.): Did you talk about Pepper's?

Charlotte (11:06 p.m.): Did you tell him he's a big baby?

Charlotte (11:07 p.m.): Did the webcam make him look even sexier?

Charlotte (11:07 p.m.): Do you miss him? Tell me all about it.

Blaire: (11:08 p.m.): It's after eleven at night, and you almost vibrated my phone right off the nightstand. I will answer two of the questions you just rapid fired at me. The meeting was short, cold and yet efficient, and no, he did not want to talk about Pepper's. He slammed the laptop shut when I asked him if he got my invitation for a drink after the next town hall since he was so big on calendar invites these days. It's almost too easy.

Charlotte (11:10 p.m.): I'm upset you chose the easiest questions to answer, but will respect the lateness of the hour. You're okay, though? I know him storming off after an almost-kiss really threw you for a loop last week.

Blaire: (11:11 p.m.): Me? Never better. I think I was just upset because the whole situation reminded me too much of you-know-who in you-know-where. I mean, I know Cole and I can't date and aren't dating, so it's not the same as that situation, but the vibes were just there. And anyway, maybe he just wanted to smell my breath in case I got stopped on the way home, but it was only one glass of wine, so I would have been fine. Maybe it wasn't an almost-kiss and I'm reading too much into it.

Blaire: (11:14 p.m.): No, it was definitely an almost-kiss, but like I said, I'm fine. It's fine.

Charlotte (11:15 p.m.): *open mouth emoji*

Blaire: (11:16 p.m.): New rule: No talking about Cole after 11:00 p.m.

Charlotte (11:17 p.m.): I mean, that's too bad, because I just came up with about ten more questions...

Blaire: (11:17 p.m.): *Blaire Greene's phone is on Do Not Disturb mode*

Charlotte (11:18 p.m.): Chicken. *Heart Emoji*

Chapter 6

July

Blaire

I got out of my car at the town square, wincing at the New England humidity already building at 8:30 in the morning. Even with the expected scorcher of a day ahead of me, I was dressed with #bosslady vibes in mind, wearing a black linen pencil skirt, a turquoise sleeveless blouse that I knew brought out the blues in my eyes and a trusty white blazer from my collection. I touched my curled hair to make sure it was laying well, using the window of the car to check out my reflection.

I tried not to overanalyze why today was the day I put the most effort into my appearance over the past month. Today, coincidentally, also happened to be the first time I'd see Cole in person since the Pepper's incident—as Charlotte and I had taken to referring to it. Our virtual meetings kept our fighting to a minimum, but it was weird having spent so much time working with him, yet not actually seeing him—or smelling him, or getting him riled up because I messed up the perfect organization on his desk, or feeling his arm brush against mine as he walked me to the door.

Cole had refused to come to Holly Ridge for any meetings until today. When I asked if we could meet in-person at the local coffee shop in Holly Ridge for a change of scenery, he muttered something about "having the high ground" and I dropped it, choosing to save my battles for what actually mattered—the festival itself.

I felt my shoulders tighten as I thought about Cole sitting behind his desk, looking like a hot, stern, tight-ass, going over whatever issue he had with my plans and suggestions that week.

Hot, stern, tight-ass? Focus, Greene. I shook myself, needing to get any such thoughts out of my head before Cole arrived on the scene. Sure, I thought maybe he was going to kiss me in the Pepper's parking lot, and I had noticed his brown eyes had gold flecks in them when we were all up-close and personal for those ten seconds, but then he fled. So, his admittedly well-formed rear end didn't deserve any more of my thoughts because it obviously belonged to someone incapable of talking about his feelings. Besides, even though I was annoyed by his response to the incident, I knew a personal relationship between us was off-limits.

I had just made my way to the gazebo in the town square when I heard a door shut behind me. I'm not quite sure how I knew from that door slam Cole had been the one to shut it, but I did.

Sure enough, I heard Cole's deep voice from behind me. "Where are these vendors? I thought you said we were meeting at 8:30?"

I steeled myself for today's battle and turned to meet his gaze. His furrowed brow was a bit dewy, thanks to that humidity and the long-sleeved button-down he insisted on wearing, despite the 90-degree high the day promised. I absolutely did not think about how that fully covered arm had looked tucking my hair behind my ear, or how he had inhaled when his nose brushed behind my ear, taking in my scent. Instead, I took a deep breath and prepared myself for a very, *very* long morning.

"I have a different meeting set for every forty-five minutes this morning, starting at 9:00. I suggested *we* meet at 8:30, I never said that was when the first vendor would be here."

Cole looked annoyed as his detail-oriented mind replayed our communications around today's meeting. When he realized I was right and our proposed vendors weren't actually late, his mouth settled into a firm line that showed he wasn't going to admit he was wrong.

I decided to take my wins where I could get them.

"So, to review, today we're meeting with the company that will rent us stalls for the Holiday Market, which we will set up here in the town square, and then the company that can build a small ice rink in one of the parking lots across the street. That's all you need to be here for. I have a few meetings after that, but none that need to involve you."

Cole nodded once, pulling out his tablet from his tan messenger bag, presumably to retrieve the detailed reports I had prepared on both vendors, the budget and estimated revenue from both the market and the ice-skating rink, and the schedule for setup and open hours once the festival started. If there was one thing I loved, it was a good report that referenced a flawless spreadsheet.

Cole looked back up at me.

"I'm still concerned about the feasibility of a temporary ice-skating rink and whether that's a good financial investment—"

"I know you're concerned about it, Cole. You've only brought it up every week for the past month, but I've worked with this vendor for other events I've planned, so he's giving us a free evaluation and estimate. You can't argue with free, can you?"

Cole looked like he was ready to, but we were saved by Benny and Julie, the owners of Merry Markets and Stalls, approaching us from their company van.

It was showtime. I was ready to show Cole how I was going to save Holly Ridge with my extremely competent, well-thought out, and yet festive Christmas festival. Merry Markets, at the raw-numbers level, appeared a bit more expensive than some of the other companies who did the same work, but they also included the decorating of their market stalls in the price, which meant they would look fantastic, and we wouldn't have to source decorations or local individuals to do it instead.

I greeted Benny and Julie, and showed them the area of the town square where we hoped to set up the market and talked through with them the best way to maximize the area available given the different sizes of stalls they had available. All the while, Cole walked behind us, taking notes on his tablet, only interjecting when prices or costs came up. Soon enough, Benny and Julie had what they needed to send us a formal proposal and promised to have that in both our inboxes within two weeks.

I looked at my watch after they drove away and noticed that we had ten minutes before Rick from Ice, Ice Baby Rinks arrived.

"I'm going to run over to Jitters to get an iced coffee before our next appointment. Can I get you . . . any . . . thing?"

Cole had finally decided the heat was too much and unbuttoned his shirt sleeves. Rolling them up, he displayed surprisingly muscled forearms for a number cruncher. I noticed my mouth was a little extra dry when I realized Cole was scoffing at my offer.

"No, thanks. I got coffee before I left Winterberry Glen. No need for any Holly Ridge coffee here."

I rolled my eyes at his blatant town snobbery.

"May I remind you that Jitters is going to supply the cookies for the cookie decorating events throughout the festival? Don't you want a chance to ask Susie about the cost of eggs and flour for the cookies?"

This was a jab at an earlier argument we had over the price Susie had quoted me for cookies, during which Cole wondered out loud if we should ask food vendors to detail their wholesale costs to ensure the markup was at a reasonable rate. I had shut that down, reminding him that all the food vendors were local and wanted the town to be saved; they weren't going to use this as a chance to price gouge. Cole's brown eyes turned harder at my jab, and he turned around to sit on a bench by the gazebo, not bothering to respond to me. I rolled my eyes again and made my way across the street to Jitters.

"Morning, Susie!" I called as I entered the coffee shop that had bordered the town square for as long as I could remember.

"Can I get a large iced coffee to go?" pulling out my wallet to pay.

Susie waved away my money. "I can see you out there meeting with that Winterberry Glen official on Christmas festival business. This one is on me."

I knew better than to argue with Susie when she was trying to be giving, so I put a few dollars in the tip jar instead.

"How's that all going anyway?" Susie asked, as she mixed in the perfect amount of oat milk and flavored syrup—after being home for over four months, Susie was well aware of my iced coffee preferences.

"We're meeting with a few vendors today, and then I'm doing an interview with a blog that highlights small-town events and festivals—trying to get the word out about our new features as soon as possible."

I left out how aggravating and overbearing it was to have to run everything by a double checker from Winterberry Glen, trying to keep a positive face when I was talking about the festival prep to anyone in town. Everyone was worried about us losing the charter and was willing to pitch in however they could. I didn't want to make anxieties worse by being anything less than mistletoe and starlight when representing the festival back to the town.

Susie handed me my iced coffee.

"I'm glad to hear things are going well and moving forward. I was worried when I hadn't seen you two around town yet."

I was more than worried when I realized Cole no longer wanted to breathe the same recycled air as me after the Pepper's incident, I thought to myself.

"We've been meeting in his office in Winterberry Glen, or virtually mostly. Before now, it's been a lot of planning and spreadsheets and cold-calling. Now that we're five months out, we'll have to be in Holly Ridge working more often."

Susie nodded. "Well, just let me know if I can do anything more than provide the cookies for the cookie decorating. The festival is always so huge for business for us. I'm already looking for extra help, so we can have everyone trained up for the festival."

I tried not to let my shoulders tighten any more than they were. This reminder of how important the festival was to the small businesses of Holly Ridge only added to the pressure to have a successful event. Sipping my coffee, I looked out the window and almost spit it right back out. Rick had pulled up while I was chatting with Susie and was now talking to Cole from his truck window.

"Ah! Thanks so much for the coffee, Susie!" I practically shouted as I ran out the door.

I do not need those two alone together for any longer than necessary. I could already imagine they would not get along.

Chapter 7

Cole

I had barely slept last night, knowing what today would bring. I had avoided being in person with Blaire after I had almost given into the temptation of her soft lips, gorgeous eyes, appealing smell —*well, it's clear why I had done so, right*? I knew as the festival approached, I wouldn't be able to keep pushing her off on virtual meetings. So, here I was, facing the heat of a New England summer morning, time spent in Holly Ridge, and of course, more time spent with Blaire.

So, even though I could have really used a coffee when Blaire asked if she could get me anything from Jitters, I found myself responding with a sarcastic comment about the quality of coffee found in Holly Ridge. I probably deserved the eye roll that response got me, but I didn't need to find myself indebted to Blaire for anything, even just a few bucks for a cup of cold coffee.

Just five more months, I thought to myself. This whole county will be in my rearview mirror in just five more months.

I was having to keep my eye on the prize. Working so closely with someone from Holly Ridge, and on the Christmas festival at that, was turning out to be a bit harder than I thought it would be. Blaire's professional-yet-somehow-super-sexy blazers weren't nearly as tantalizing through a computer monitor and seeing them in person definitely didn't help one bit.

As I sat there sweating in the town square, I was just about to follow Blaire into Jitters to buy my own iced coffee when a pickup truck with "Ice, Ice Baby Rinks" in huge vinyl letters on the side pulled up alongside where I was sitting.

"Hey, bro," the driver greeted me, a land-locked surfer dude wearing what used to be a t-shirt, with the sleeves cut off to reveal his arms and part of his side and a baseball cap backward. "Are you the numbers dude working with Blaire on the Holly Ridge festival?"

I blinked slowly at him. "If by numbers dude, you mean Cole Thomas, the Winterberry Glen CFO, then yes, that's me."

The driver smirked.

"Blaire said I'd recognize you as the only guy wearing a long-sleeved button-down and khakis in the town square during a heat wave. I'm Rick, owner of Ice, Ice Baby Rinks, the portable ice rink vendor Blaire's considering for the festival. Let me park and I'll be right with you."

I watched the truck pull away, not sure whether to focus on the fact that Blaire was describing my clothing choices to one of our potential vendors or the fact that I doubted this guy could identify any water forms that didn't exist at the beach, let alone create a portable ice rink.

I was stewing about surfer boy Rick when Blaire came rushing back across the street, iced coffee in hand, moving way too quickly for someone wearing a white blazer and carrying a cup of coffee capable of staining it.

"Hi! Guys! I see you've met! Rick, Cole. Cole, Rick."

Blaire was practically shouting at us as she approached, joining me in the town square at the same time as Rick. Her face was flushed, but I wasn't sure if that was from the heat, her 100-meter coffee dash, or something else.

"Blaire Bear!" Rick exclaimed, and grabbed Blaire around the waist, spinning her in a circle, again endangering her white blazer. *Why was I so obsessed with her blazers?*

He returned her to the ground.

"You look good! Though, you always look good." Rick winked at Blaire, apparently ignoring proper business meeting decorum. "Glad to see being back in Holly Ridge is treating you well."

Back in Holly Ridge? I thought to myself. He knows her well enough to know where she's from?

Blaire looked up at me and, seeming to read my mind, explained.

"Rick and I have worked together on a bunch of winter festivals all over the tristate area over the past several years. He's the best in the portable ice rink business, and luckily runs his business out of the next county over, so he's able to get us a rink without any time on a waiting list."

"I make my own refrigerant and brine mixtures that set the ice in record time," Rick added in. "Not that we usually have trouble in New England winters, but global warming is real, and we need to be ready for anything! The patent is pending on my mixture. I'm hoping to sell it to other companies to improve the ice rink game in general, and then get back in the lab to see what I can cook up next."

I just blinked at them both, stunned by Rick's chemistry prowess and by the way Blaire championed him. I hadn't seen her do that with any of the vendors we had discussed yet.

Is there some sort of history between them? Is that the kind of guy Blaire goes for?

"Great, awesome." I replied, aware that my tone was clipped. "Let's show Rick where the parking lot is you want the rink in, so I can get out of this heat." Wanting to be done with this meeting had nothing to do with me not wanting to watch Blaire and Rick together. Nothing at all.

Blaire glared at me for my tone, but nonetheless turned away and walked next to Rick toward the parking lot right across from the town square. I tried not to notice how Rick threw his arm around Blaire's shoulders as they walked, making small talk. Her body language relaxed in a way it had never been during any of our meetings, except maybe across the table at Pepper's.

Guess that *is* her type then.

After Rick declared the parking lot location "totally rad" for one of his best rinks, he got ready to head to his next consult.

"I'll send you a proposal by next week for the rink we discussed, with the Blaire Bear discount thrown in."

I felt my eyes threaten to move into one of Blaire's signature eye rolls, but I kept my poise. I felt her eyes on me as I watched him get in his truck to leave.

"Okay, let's have it."

She squared her shoulders like she was ready to battle over Rick and his rink.

Where to start? The fact that your apparent ex-something is one of our vendors?

"The Blaire Bear discount?" I asked her. "You know you're not supposed to be using the town's situation in advertising— that goes for securing discounts as well. I also don't think the state would appreciate you using personal connections with exes to get discounts, either."

"The Blaire Bear discount," her cheeks flushing pink as she said that ridiculous phrase out loud, "is nothing new. I've brought in Rick's rinks to every town I've worked with on their winter festivals over the past seven years. I'm happy to show you contracts that reflect the same discount if you think it's going to be an issue with the state. And, not that my personal life is any of your business, but Rick has been with his partner, *Steve*, since college. We had to sit with one of his rinks overnight because of a potential rain issue at a festival and he heard my dad call me Blaire Bear on the phone. He thought it was hilarious, so he took on the nickname too."

I felt something loosen in my chest I hadn't even realized was tight when I realized Rick wasn't an ex-anything of Blaire's, but it felt good to fight with her in-person again.

"I still don't think it's a good idea to take up the largest parking area near the town square with an ice rink."

If possible, Blaire's chin raised even higher as she took a step closer, brandishing her clipboard as a buffer between us.

"We've been through this, Cole. We don't want cars coming through the town square, anyway. I'm going to petition the City Council to make the streets around the square pedestrian only during the festival's open hours. We'll be very clear in advertising that the festival is walkable, and we'll have handicap parking available. It's a much better use of that square of pavement to have an attraction than to fill it with cars and create gridlock with people trying to see if they can snag a spot."

Maybe it's because we were physically standing in the town square, but I could see her point about the gridlock. Having a fully walkable festival would be safer and more visually appealing and keeping the road closures to festival hours would still allow the businesses along the square to receive their deliveries in the early morning hours.

Begrudgingly, I admitted, "Okay, I see your point. If Rick can give us a workable financial proposal and I decide to approve it, the rink can go in the parking lot. No more arguments from me."

I could tell Blaire wanted to smack me with that clipboard at reminding her I had final financial approval over her entire festival plan, but instead her eyes fixed onto something behind me.

"Oh! That's Tanya! She's, like, an hour early! Shit, I thought I had more time before she arrived."

I turned around to watch a blond woman confidently walk toward us wearing wedge sandals, a sundress, and the largest hat I had ever seen balanced on her head. The woman, who I now knew as Tanya, wiggled her fingers at us and yelled "Yoo-hoo!" across the square.

"Who's this again? I thought it was just the two vendors this morning."

"You were only on the schedule to meet the two vendors this morning," Blaire murmured out of the side of her mouth as Tanya approached. "Tanya is the most influential small-town blogger in New England. I've been working to get her to cover Holly Ridge's festival since I took the job in March. She finally agreed to see the town today."

I wasn't quite sure how a festival blogger could make the usually cool and professional Blaire so nervous, but this was something I had to stick around to see.

I heard Blaire take a deep breath. "Tanya! So good to see you!"

She locked in what I had come to recognize as her professional smile—*when did I start cataloging her smiles?*—and reached out to shake Tanya's hand.

"Welcome to Holly Ridge!"

"Thank you, dear," Tanya replied.

"I wasn't so sure about covering Holly Ridge after the last few festivals had been a flop, but when I heard they had brought in Blaire Greene to run the show, I knew I had to give it another chance. And lucky me I did. Look at the sights there are to see."

She finished this last statement looking directly at me. I felt myself wanting to laugh at her boldness, but instead managed to stick my hand out to shake hers.

"Cole Thomas, Winterberry Glen CFO. I'm working with Ms. Greene on the festival."

I chanced a glance at Blaire to see how she was reacting to Tanya alluding that I was one of the best sights to see in her precious hometown. Blaire looked flabbergasted for a second, but quickly recovered.

"That's Holly Ridge. Always full of surprises! I'm so glad to be back in my hometown running this festival. It's a dream come true for me."

Apparently, Blaire felt the need to really lay it on thick with Tanya. I had never heard her use this syrupy tone before.

"We weren't expecting you until closer to lunchtime," Blaire continued. "I was planning to take you over to Joe's Café, just across the square there, for some iced teas and lunch to talk all about the festival."

"Well," Tanya replied. "I'm here now. Maybe Cole should join us for a pre-lunch cocktail, and we can really dive in to the numbers side of things, as well as talking about the festival."

I jumped on this opening.

"I would love to join you ladies for lunch. It will be great to hear Blaire explain the festival to someone other than me for once."

I could feel Blaire's eye-daggers driving into my temple, but I chose to ignore her, addressing Tanya directly. "Shall we?"

Tanya tucked her arm into mine, which I felt was a little much, and immediately launched into questions about my job as CFO as we walked toward the café. Blaire had no choice but to follow behind us—she wouldn't miss her chance to show off Holly Ridge to Tanya by refusing a direct request from the blogger herself. I could feel her glare on my back, adding an extra few degrees of heat to the day the whole way to the restaurant.

Chapter 8

Blaire

Furiously, I walked behind Cole and Tanya, keeping less distance than what was considered polite, but there was absolutely no way I was going to miss out on a word of what was said between them. It took me weeks to get Tanya to even reply to my emails, and even more time to get her to agree to come to Holly Ridge to hear about our festival, and there was no way Cole Thomas was going to screw this up.

As we walked toward Joe's Café, Tanya's arm tucked in between Cole's annoyingly firm bicep and those exposed forearms, Tanya questioned him about being a small-town CFO. Her high-pitched giggle at every other answer started to grate on my nerves, and I was once again glad for the fact that most local businesses were only a stone's throw from the town square.

"Here we are! Joe's Café!"

I saw Cole jump, which gave me a smidge of smug satisfaction, and I spared him a smirk before putting on my press-conference-ready smile to address Tanya.

"Tanya, I think you're just going to love Joe's. He's kept all the town favorites on the menu from when I was growing up, but he has also added a lot of new foods and cocktails to keep up with the Joneses. We don't want anyone to leave town for their quinoa and organic cocktails!"

I watched Cole as my jab landed. He knew I was referring to Muggsie's, which I knew was his favorite restaurant due to the paper coasters and free pens he had on his office desk. Needing to expend some energy after receiving one too many passive-aggressive emails from Cole in a day, I had done some research and found out their menu hadn't updated in years. I saved that information for a moment just like this one.

"I asked Joe to reserve us an umbrella table outside. The covered roof and ceiling fans really make the July heat almost pleasant, and then we won't be freezing in the overcompensating AC."

Maybe I was laying it on a bit thick, but my nature desired everything go according to plan and wouldn't let me have it any other way. I needed Tanya to be in a good mood for this conversation, and not only did that involve the perfect seating arrangement but also meant we'd have Cole Thomas join us for lunch as well.

"Perfect!" Tanya responded. "I hate when restaurants are too cold. It totally ruins the experience for me."

I knew that. I planned this afternoon down to the T, but what I hadn't planned for was Cole butting in and throwing everything off.

I said hello to Meghan—Joe's daughter, serving as hostess while home from college for the summer—and asked for our table reservation. I had let Joe know that this meeting involved some great publicity for the festival, so even though we were an hour early, I knew the staff would make it work for us.

"Sure thing, Blaire!" Meghan responded. "We have your table ready. Just let me grab an extra set of silverware and I'll take you right out!"

Meghan's eyes lingered appreciatively on Cole as she grabbed the rolled silverware from behind the hostess stand, because apparently women appreciating Cole's looks was the theme of the hour. I couldn't blame them. He did know how to wear a pair of khakis, but I also did not need to be reminded of how Cole's ass looked in the most boring pants on earth. I needed to focus. I didn't care that other women were looking at him, no not at all.

Seated at our table on the patio, Tanya acknowledged that the ambiance was perfect and picked up her drink menu, taking her time to look through all the summery options Joe had put on as specials for the season.

"I think it's a sangria type of day. How about you all?"

Tanya laid her menu down and looked at both of us expectantly.

"I think that sounds great!" I responded, promising myself I would just have one small glass and then switch to water.

"Just water for me, I think," Cole replied, nose buried in his food menu, much to Tanya's apparent dismay.

Tanya was a beautiful woman, and I shouldn't be surprised that she was interested in Cole. Even if he was infuriating, and you know, the kind of guy that runs away after an almost-kiss in a parking lot. I could understand her interest in him, but I hated how much it was bothering me.

Assuring myself that I wasn't going to be the type of woman who thought poorly of another successful and attractive single woman for taking note of an attractive single man, I made eye contact with our server, and we placed our drink orders. It was time to put thoughts of Cole and any woman who may find him interesting to the side and put my focus on Tanya, her blog, and taking another step toward saving Holly Ridge.

Chapter 9

Cole

I could tell that Blaire was determined to get this meeting back on track. For a moment, I felt something a lot like remorse for throwing her off her meticulously planned schedule, which morphed into wondering how else I could fluster Blaire, which led dangerously close to remembering the last time I had left Blaire caught off guard. What would happen if I brushed my leg against hers under the table? Good lord, did I need to get laid.

When I tuned back into the conversation, I realized Tanya was asking Blaire about her childhood experiences growing up in Holly Ridge and going to the festivals.

"It was my favorite time of year, not that I really had much choice being the mayor's daughter," Blaire was saying, "but it was more than that. It was the way the whole town came together to celebrate something and welcome in the visitors who came from all over to celebrate what the town does best."

Suddenly both women were looking at me, one look full of intrigue and one full of murderous intent. I must not have swallowed my scoff as well as I thought I had.

"You haven't had the same experience at the Holly Ridge festival since being Winterberry Glen's CFO, Cole?" Tanya asked me. At this I realized that the wedge heels and sangria ordering before lunch may be a front to lull her subjects into complacency. Tanya didn't miss much.

While I didn't relish giving Blaire any insight into my history, I found myself needing to answer honestly.

"I grew up in Winterberry Glen, so my history with the festival dates back even further, but I haven't attended the festival since I was ten years old when it was made clear to me that, while visitors from far and wide may be welcome in Holly Ridge for the festival, someone from Winterberry Glen was not."

"Ah yes," Tanya stirred her straw in the rapidly melting ice in her glass, having finished her beverage already. "The famous feud."

"I don't know that I would call it famous!" Blaire exclaimed, her eyes flashing steely blue and wide, her voice increasing in pitch. "It's just hard to have two towns so close together—it's like siblings, you know! They fight. My sister and I fought all the time growing up. It's hard feeling like one's constantly being compared to the other, not knowing if you'll ever live up to expectations. Will the relationship ever change, or is it too broken?"

I picked up my water glass to prevent any unintentional reactions from sneaking out of me this time, while Blaire clamped her mouth shut, realizing she may have completely overcompensated by trying to divert Tanya away from the feud.

Tanya was distracted by the arrival of the waiter with another glass of sangria and our lunch orders. Blaire still looked flustered but seemed relieved to have been saved from more feud discussion and that her unintentional admission appeared to have gone unnoticed.

Even though we had just come very close to a deep wound I tried to keep hidden, I felt I needed to throw Blaire a bone to help turn things around. After all, I didn't want Blaire using sympathy to sell the festival with the media, but I also didn't want the state audit office to catch wind of any childish behavior between us.

"Blaire really does have a vision for an updated festival,

though. She's being very intentional in the vendors she's bringing in, ensuring their operations are as green as possible and being sure to support local and diverse owners and companies whenever possible," I offered as Tanya drizzled dressing on her salad. Blaire paused with her soup spoon halfway to her mouth, a puzzled look on her face, as if she was trying to figure out where I was headed with this.

I give her a small nod, which seems to reset her circuits, and the poised, pulled-together festival planner is with us again.

"That's right," Blaire continued, setting her spoon down and launching into the spiel I knew by heart now—it being listed at the front of every schedule draft we'd been through in the past four months. "While there are vendors that have been traditionally used for the festival, I'm trying to be sure that our vendor list is inclusive and local whenever it's possible. This starts with the Tree Lighting Ceremony and the Holiday Market at the beginning of the festival and wraps up with the Gingerbread Ball on New Year's Eve. We're also trying to acknowledge other traditions and cultures along the way as well. It ended up having to be a more minor part of this year's planning with timing and festival constraints—a menorah in the square near the gazebo, for example—but I hope to expand it in future years. Who knows, maybe someday it will be the Holly Ridge Holiday Festival instead of the Holly Ridge Christmas Festival." Blaire's conviction and pride in the work she's put into the festival was apparent on her face, and it was impossible for me to look away from her. Her passion just enhanced her beauty.

"That sounds like it will be really great. The town is super cute and the festival schedule you sent over looks to be full of interesting events and traditions," Tanya replied, putting her napkin on top of her salad bowl, and after placing her hand on my arm, she looked up at me. "Now, I think I just need a bit more information from Cole here, and I'll be all set for my article."

I glanced across the table at Blaire to see her glaring at Tanya's hand, where it rested on my bare arm. If Blaire's eyes contained laser beams, she would have burned a hole right through both of us, and while her disdain made me want to shake the offending hand off, I pretended to not notice and responded directly to Tanya.

"I'd be glad to take a stroll around the square with you. Perhaps we can stop in at Jitters for an after-lunch coffee on the way back to your car?"

Tanya smiled before standing, wavering slightly when she was out of her chair.

"Perfect. I'll just use the little girl's room and be right back!"

Blaire sat with her arms crossed and eyebrow cocked. I sighed, knowing she wasn't going to be pleased with my offer to walk Tanya to her car.

"What is it, Blaire?"

"Oh, nothing," her voice barely louder than a whisper. "Just so glad you had to tag along on this lunch with me, for God knows what reason. But now you can take her to get Jitters coffee, which you were too good for two hours ago, and 'walk her to her car' all by yourself? Just wondering how that double standard looks from your pedestal."

Was that jealousy I heard in Blaire's voice? Considering I had to lean in to hear her, catching a whiff of her signature scent, I couldn't be sure if what I heard was jealousy or anger for messing up her lunch.

I tried to keep my voice impassive as I responded, matching her voice's volume, keeping my head inclined toward hers.

"I don't know if you noticed, but Tanya consumed several glasses of sangria and only ate half of her salad, and she drove here. I'm killing some time, trying to see if she'll sober up and getting some coffee in her to counteract the alcohol before she gets behind the wheel. It usually works, but if it doesn't, I'll take her back to Winterberry Glen and she can sleep it off in my office."

I regretted adding the "it usually works" to my last statement, as something in Blaire's expression—as she sat back in her chair— let me know she saw more than I wanted her to, that this wasn't the first time I watched someone sober up or need a nap before getting behind the wheel.

Tanya chose that moment to return to the table. "Ready to go, handsome?"

"You bet I am. Now why don't you tell me all about this blog of yours?" I stood up, grabbing her bag and letting her tuck her arm in mine.

Tanya started a long-winded explanation, as I knew she would, and we headed toward the entrance of Joe's and back into the heat. Against my better judgment, I looked over my shoulder at Blaire as we exited the café and saw her watching us go. We made eye contact for one moment, her face a mix of emotions I couldn't quite name in a brief glance, before I broke the connection and turned back to the town square.

Chapter 10

Blaire

It was becoming a bit of a pattern that Cole left me behind recalibrating. It's not something I'm incredibly comfortable with. I enjoy my feelings of certainty, and Cole seems to have a way to upend those more and more every time we are together. The way he observed and cared for Tanya made me wonder what other depths and complexities he kept hidden, but I sighed and resigned myself to the fact that I may never know them.

After settling our bill for lunch, I walked to the other side of the town square to pop into Ridge Reads to visit Charlotte. I promised her I would debrief her after my in-person meetings with Cole and lunch with Tanya. She would absolutely get a kick out of the fact that the two had bled over into each other.

I walked into the bookstore and took a deep breath, letting the smell of books and memories of years growing up in this town staple wash over me. Charlotte smiled at me from behind the counter.

"It's about time! I've been waiting for you to get here to take my lunch. I'm starving! Mitch, I'm taking my lunch! Come cover the counter!"

After Mitch arrived at the counter and Charlotte briefed him on the projects she was in the middle of, she bounced around the edge, grabbed my hand, and pulled me back to our favorite armchairs, tucked away in the back corner of the store.

"Okay, sit down," Charlotte ordered me. "I'm going to go grab my food out of the fridge. When I get back, I want to know what he was wearing, how he greeted you, and if he finally addressed the Pepper's incident, in that order, please."

"Awesome, great, fantastic, just what I want to think about when it comes to my pain-in-the-ass festival overlord, Char. Grab me a Diet Coke to help ease the pain?"

I knew Charlotte would see right through my good-natured complaining after so many years of friendship, and I considered while she was gone if I should lie, to both Charlotte and myself, about the amount of times I had glanced at Cole's forearms. I mean, I could describe the color and pattern of his shirt in great detail.

Charlotte returned with her salad and Diet Cokes for both of us, flopping into her seat and saying in her lovingly demanding tone, "Okay, now spill."

"He was wearing long-sleeves and khakis in this heat, he greeted me in a completely crotchety way about the schedule, and he definitely didn't even attempt to address the Pepper's incident. I mean, it never really even crossed my mind either," I responded, stopping for a sip of that sweet, sweet, so-bad-for-me-but-tastes-so-good nectar of life. At the look Charlotte leveled at me, I felt the need to revise my last answer.

"Okay, maybe I was thinking about it before he showed up, when I wondered how he would act around me, and then maybe once more when he rolled his sleeves up and flashed me those fore-arms, but that's all I'm giving you on that. I focused on fighting for my preferred vendors and trying not to freak out when he decided to come to lunch with Tanya after she showed up early."

"Wait. He crashed your lunch with Tanya? Was he trying to snoop on the angle you were taking with the press on the festival?"

Charlotte was working on a public relations degree at the local college in the limited free time she got from the store, so she always used my work stories as case studies for what she was learning.

"I hadn't even thought of that possibility, honestly. I thought he was just being a giant turd-face and wanting to get under my skin. Especially after he conceded that my location for the ice rink was a better idea than his," I said, thinking back to the self-satisfied smirk he had leveraged my way when he accepted Tanya's invitation.

"So, how did that all go? Did he derail the interview? Do you think the blog post is still going to be okay?" Charlotte rapid-fire responded, her finished salad container discarded on the side table next to us.

"Well, Tanya was really laying on the charm thick, and he didn't really seem to rebuff her advances," which made Charlotte's eyebrows shoot up toward her hairline. "But that's totally fine. They're both attractive and single individuals, and he's obviously decided to pretend the Pepper's incident didn't happen, so it's fine." *Fine*. What a word! It can hold many different meanings within four simple letters.

"Tanya asked a few questions about the feud, which Cole was sort of helpful in deflecting—thank God, the towns' feuding does *not* need to be the story—and then he was actually complimentary about my efforts for inclusivity and green actions! I dunno, it was a really weird lunch that ended with him taking her to coffee, so she didn't get into her car right away after having had a few glasses of Joe's sangria."

"Wow! Wait, he left *with* her after lunch?" Charlotte wasn't about to let that nugget slip on by. "That douche-nozzle. Moving in on a blogger . . ."

"No, no, I really don't think it was like that," I responded, before Charlotte got any ideas about retaliation.

"He honestly seemed like he was just concerned about her driving, and not that he was interested in any one-on-one time with her off the record. I do think having had him there is going to be a good thing for the blog post in general. Other than some standard anti-Holly Ridge snobbery, it was overall a successful day."

"Well, good," Charlotte responded, gathering up her lunch remnants and my now empty can of soda. "I know you were nervous about the interview, so I'm glad to hear it went well and that the unexpected appearance of Cole didn't mess things up too badly. Do you think he'll be back to avoiding meeting with you in person now, or will he be a bit more normal that the post-Pepper's seal has been broken?"

"We didn't really get a chance to talk about our next meeting with the way the day worked itself out," I realized. "But I think he's not going to be able to get away with pushing us back to virtual as much. Things are going to start to heat up and we'll need to start meeting with volunteers and vendors."

"Heat up, huh?" Charlotte winked at me as she clung to my unintentional word choice. "Well, my hope is the heat ratchets itself up to ghost pepper heat and not just Pepper's parking lot heat." She looked pleased with herself for her Dad joke.

I snorted and rolled my eyes at her.

"Go back to work. I'm going to stay here and follow-up with the vendors we met with today and get a jump on making my to-do list for next week. I'm honestly surprised Cole didn't ask me for it first thing this morning."

"Maybe he was too busy thinking about a certain parking lot almost-kiss himself," she said as she walked away snickering.

Just you wait, Charlotte, I thought to myself as I opened my laptop and dug into getting myself set up for next week. What goes around definitely comes around.

Chapter 11

Cole

After a few cups of coffee, some spins around the Holly Ridge square, and more conversation about blogs and the direction Tanya hoped to take hers in than I honestly thought two humans could have, Tanya departed for her drive home, pouting slightly about my refusal to share my personal number with her "for any further quotes or questions" she might have. I felt a bit bad about mixing signals to get her to stay so she'd have time to sober up, but I felt much better about her being behind the wheel now than I did right after lunch. I told myself that the real reason I gave her only my business card was because she was involved with the festival and had nothing to do with the way Blaire had looked at Tanya's hand on my arm during lunch.

The day had completely gotten away from me, but luckily, Friday was a remote workday for me, so I hadn't missed any meetings or anything that I couldn't catch up on over the weekend. I was due at my mom's house for dinner with her and Austin in thirty minutes, and I would just have time to stop and pick up the food I had ordered during a blog-talk bathroom break earlier this afternoon.

As I drove back across the river, the memories of my mom

trying to stop my dad from driving after too much to drink finally crept back in after being held at bay all day. I was a lot more successful at charming Tanya into delaying her trip than mom often was with dad when I was growing up. He had called her all sorts of names, accusing her of killing his buzz and being a worry wart—couched in much harsher terms, much too harsh for someone you had once promised to love and to cherish. Mom had bounced back some from the emotional abuse since he left, but she still preferred to stay within the confines of my childhood home whenever she could. These weekly dinners with her were something I started after college, even though I saw her several other times a week, and Austin joined us when he could, having become a surrogate son.

Armed with bags of hot food, some fresh-cut flowers from the florist next door to the restaurant and a six-pack of Austin's favorite IPA, I opened the kitchen door to hear the two of them already in the living room laughing over something. I put my phone and keys down in the kitchen before I approached the living room cautiously. Austin's favorite topics to make my mom laugh were his outrageous dating stories, or worse, stories about me.

"What's so funny in here?"

I crossed into the room from the kitchen, not able to stop myself from smiling at the grin on my mom's face while she sat in her favorite recliner.

"Oh, just telling Mrs. T about the failed app date I went on last night. It turns out that inflammable and nonflammable are *not* the same, and I did not impress my volunteer firefighter date when I mixed them up at the restaurant."

Austin's eyes twinkled while he poked fun at himself good-naturedly. Austin was an outgoing guy, but he was sensitive underneath all that humor and I made a note to check in with him later to be sure his date's brush off over his mix-up hadn't actually hurt his feelings.

"Austin, you're such a catch. Anyone who isn't willing to

overlook something small like that was definitely going to be more trouble than they were worth in the long run. You don't need someone that judgmental in your life," my mom responded, standing up from the chair to check what food I had picked up for dinner and started getting plates and silverware for the table in the kitchen. No matter how many times I told her I could handle that, she refused to let me help set the table, saying my bringing dinner over to the house was enough.

"You're probably right, Mrs. T," Austin replied to her retreating back, turning his head to me with mischievous intent in his eyes. "I was just hoping for a little snuggle in the parking lot afterward. I hear that's all the rage these days."

I looked at Austin, wondering if murdering him would tarnish my record with the state audit office, but luckily, Mom was too busy getting dishes and a vase for the flowers out of the cabinet to respond to his targeted response.

"How was today, bro?" Austin asked, in a quieter voice that wouldn't carry into the kitchen. While he liked to rib me when he got the chance, he respected my private intentions about women around my mom. I didn't need her to get all excited that I was going to meet someone in the area, settle down, and give her any grandkids to dote on.

"It was . . . a day."

I thought about how the day started with me obsessing over yet another one of Blaire's blazers, took a sharp turn with an overly familiar, yet brainiac surfer dude turned ice-rink mastermind, and ended with an unexpected diversion in the form of a festival blogger.

"Did she bring up the parking lot incident at all?" Austin pushed, knowing mom would be calling us into the kitchen to eat any second, and like a dog chasing a bone, wasn't content to let me stay completely mum.

"No, of course not," I responded. "I think it's pretty clear it was a near miss, and that there's a whole host of reasons we didn't actually kiss that night."

"Oh, you mean because you bolted mid-lean and then haven't had the stones to see her in person since?" Austin said, not bothering to sugarcoat anything.

I groaned into my hands, being forced to remember again how I had just left her shell-shocked in the parking lot without a word. "What was I supposed to do? Be an emotionally well-adjusted adult and talk about how we almost did the one thing the state audit office indicated could screw up my position with them next year? Yeah, I don't think so. Especially because it makes no sense I would want to kiss her, since she annoys the daylights out of me on a regular basis. And anyway, I'm sure she doesn't want to talk about it anymore than I do."

Her priority was the festival and saving Holly Ridge and mine was leaving Winterberry Glen and my past in the rearview mirror. Even if the state office hadn't laid down the rules regarding our personal relationship, it could never work. At that cheery thought, Mom called us into the kitchen, and I turned my attention to one of my favorite hours of the week.

Chapter 11.5

To: BGreene@hollyridge.gov
From: Charlotte@ridgereads.com
Date: July 15 9:56 a.m.
Subject: Glowing Review... of you?

Hi B-

Presumably you already have Tanya's blog post memorized since it went up early this morning, but just wanted to be 100 percent sure the following bit was sticking out for you.

"I had a chance to speak with Cole Thomas, Winterberry Glen CFO, about his colleague in festival planning, Blaire Greene, and how she came about the job. Small town politics can be rife with nepotism, but Cole insists Blaire deserves the chance she's getting with Holly Ridge's Christmas festival based on her own merit, saying 'Ms. Greene works harder and cares more about this 16-day festival than I've seen city leaders work on and care for their agenda for the whole city for the entire year. I have no doubts that if Holly Ridge does not keep its charter, that it will not be due to any faults on the part of Ms. Greene. If I liked Christmas or small-town festivals, she would be who I would want in charge.'"

Love, C.

To: Charlotte@ridgereads.com
From: BGreene@hollyridge.gov
Date: July 15 10:16 a.m.
Subject: Re: Glowing Review... of you?

Hi C-

I have read the article several times. I'm overall happy with it. I can't believe she's adding Holly Ridge to her festivals to watch list. It's going to be great exposure for us. I do wish she wouldn't have quoted Cole directly, but I guess the quote is nice enough. Cole and I are going to need to be prepared for more feud questions from the press come December, though. It's definitely time for me to push him on getting us an appointment at the Winterberry Glen archives to get their side of the story.

Love, B

To: BGreene@hollyridge.gov
From: Charlotte@ridgereads.com
Date: July 15 10:46 a.m.
Subject: Re: Re: Glowing Review... of you?

Sweet, Naive, B-

Ohh, a date to the historical archives with the man who just said
SUCH NICE THINGS ABOUT YOU ON THE RECORD
AND YOU'RE IGNORING IT. Sounds romantic.

Deflect all you want, girlfriend. I see you.

You know you love me, C

To: Charlotte@ridgereads.com
From: BGreene@hollyridge.gov
Date: July 15 2:06 p.m.
Subject: Re: Re: Re: Glowing Review... of you?

C, you're the worst.

Dusty archives are definitely an appropriate atmosphere for a
completely platonic, work-relationship outing.
Though, will I imagine, say, Zac Efron telling me I've earned
something of my own merit while he brings me to orgasm? I
won't say the idea hasn't crossed my mind.

Love you, B.

To: BGreene@hollyridge.gov
From: Charlotte@ridgereads.com
Date: July 15 2:45 p.m.
Subject: Dusty...

And full of cobwebs, like some other part of your anatomy. *side-eye*

Sorry, I couldn't resist. First glass of wine tonight at Joe's is on me. We're celebrating this successful article.

Love you too, C.

Chapter 12

October

Cole

After putting Blaire off for six months on her request to get access to the Winterberry Glen archives to investigate the origin of the feud, I finally gave in and set up a meeting with Mrs. Sanderson, the town librarian and archivist. I had to use all my charm to get Mrs. Sanderson to agree to meet with Blaire—considering her origins. My mom believed the only reason she gave in was because she wanted to meet the girl I was "trying so hard for," but if Mrs. Sanderson had Blaire in her inbox and on her phone every day, she'd wear down eventually, too.

Blaire and I met in person more regularly since the meetings around the festival were getting more practical and involved more people. I managed not to be alone with her yet, but I knew Mrs. Sanderson's style was to pull out the records and microfiche and leave people to their research. As I walked down the sidewalk to the front door of the library and spotted Blaire, hair shiny and curled, wearing a mustard blazer with a maroon scarf and somehow managing to not look like a hot dog condiment cart, I wondered if it was too late to bail.

Blaire spotted me and raised her hand in a wave, a smile

brightening her face, presumably at the prospect of doing research and not because I was in her line of sight. Something had changed in our relationship since Tanya's post had come out. Maybe it was the fact that I appeared protective of Blaire. Perhaps it was just the fact that Blaire was happy it was creating a positive buzz around the festival with Tanya's audience and beyond. Regardless, we were definitely friendlier and less antagonistic. Nothing like discussing our town's histories and feud to put an end to that.

I nodded to her as I walked up.

"Greene."

"Thomas. Are you ready to do this?"

"I'd rather get a root canal."

"Awe, that's the spirit. Too bad, let's go inside!"

Chuckling in spite of myself, I followed her into the library. She walked up to the circulation counter, opened her mouth to speak, and then realized I made the appointment. She closed her mouth again and looked at me expectantly.

"Hi there, Mrs. Nuñez. We have a three o'clock with Mrs. Sanderson."

"Ah yes, of course. Our Cole and his Holly Ridge . . . colleague. I'll let her know you're here."

It was clear by the look of surprise at the ice in Mrs. Nuñez's tone that Blaire doesn't venture anywhere other than the government center when she visits our side of the river. It's not that Winterberry Glen citizens have a radar for Holly Ridge folks exactly, but Blaire isn't exactly a nobody in these parts, especially now that she's planning the festival and Tanya's blog started a wave of coverage for the town.

I stood in the library glancing around the circulation area. Not much has changed over the last few decades, including the staff. The library was a place where I felt safe, like I could hide from the drama in my house when my dad was still home, and then could escape my mom's sadness after he left.

Shaken from my melancholy walk down memory lane by the

sound of keys jangling from a key ring, I turned to see Mrs. Sanderson approaching.

"Mrs. S," I greeted her. "Thank you so much for seeing us."

"Hmph," she responded, taking in Blaire standing next to me. "Well, you know I can't say no to you, Cole. But the flower delivery certainly didn't hurt anything."

She turned and walked away without another word, the expectation that we would follow her clear from her quick movements.

Flower delivery? Blaire mouthed at me as we moved down a hallway to a stairwell.

I shook my head, hoping she'd get the message—*not now. Leave it alone.*

We continued down the stairs behind Mrs. Sanderson in silence as she led us to research room number three.

Mrs. Sanderson held the door open for us to enter and indicated we should each take a seat side by side in front of the microfiche machines and the books holding newspaper clippings.

She cleared her throat and addressed us in her no-nonsense, librarian tone.

"Now, Cole tells me you're interested in finding out more about the Holly Ridge-Winterberry Glen feud. I'm assuming you've already been through everything Holly Ridge has on the topic?"

Blaire nodded. "Yes, I have, and it really wasn't clicking for me. I mean, I get that Winterberry Glen was jealous of the Christmas festival, so they dug up and stole the town square tree. It was a crappy thing to do right before the festival started, but the mayor replaced it with a tree from up north, so I get being annoyed, but I'm not quite sure why it's lasted."

Mrs. Sanderson's scoff came at a volume that had no place in a library, causing me to jump a few inches in my chair.

"What an interesting revisionist history they have over there in your archives. Well, you'll want to start reading from left to right with the piles there. You'll see there are even copies of Holly

Ridge papers included . . . you won't be able to accuse us of only taking one side. Feel free to see yourself out."

Blaire stared at the door where Mrs. Sanderson exited, in shock.

She looked at me and asked, "Do you really think the story in Holly Ridge is that one-sided?"

"Only one way to find out, Greene. Get reading. I'll be here answering my e-mail on the trickle-slow Wi-Fi that carries into the basement. I'm just here so you can be in here. I have no desire to learn about any of this."

I pulled out my tablet and tried to focus on my e-mail—answering some questions about small-town finances and governance from Tanya, off the record, as I had found myself doing over the past few months. But as time passed, I was distracted by Blaire's body language. She was shuffling through articles almost manically, her shoulders getting tighter and tighter, until she finally let out a small scream-groan of frustration.

"What is it, Greene? What did you find?"

Blaire answered me with her eyes shut while pinching the bridge of her nose. "Well, there is one thing that the Holly Ridge archives got right. Winterberry Glen did steal the tree before the Christmas festival a hundred years ago. But they left a lot of other details out."

I waited in silence, knowing by now that Blaire would continue talking without any prompting from me when she was done processing.

"The state meant to deliver the tree for the *Winterberry Glen* Christmas Festival 125 years ago, but the towns are so close, the delivery man got on the wrong side of the river and left the tree in Holly Ridge instead. So, Holly Ridge decided to throw a Christmas festival, and the tree was such a big hit that the Winterberry Glen festival had to shut down. And if that wasn't enough, the son of the mayor of Holly Ridge stole the girlfriend of the son of the mayor of Winterberry Glen and married her. That's what drove Huck to steal the tree in the first place. If he couldn't have his girl, his girl couldn't have a Christmas festival either. That's why the mayor of Holly Ridge paid so much money to replace the tree with another one without any fuss. He knew his son was a jackass, and he had no recourse to get the tree back from Winterberry Glen. He just covered it all up, and we kept on having the festival."

Well, damn. That was worse than I could have imagined, and something I never had heard before. The answer was down here the whole time, but Winterberry Glen residents mostly just boycotted the festival because it was in Holly Ridge—not because they had stolen festival glory from us a hundred years ago.

Blaire looked so crestfallen. I felt like I had to inject some logic into the room, whether she wanted to hear it or not.

"Look, Greene, the origins suck, but that was a long time ago. And you're working on today's festival and hoping to bring it into the future. You don't have to feel guilty for working hard on something that you can change for the better. And now you know, and you can do something about it. It's when people know they're benefiting from horrible things people did before them and choose to ignore it or not fight for change that we fall apart."

Blaire nodded, and I saw the wheels turning in her head.

"Thomas, did you know about all this?"

"Nope, not at all. I'm learning right along with you."

"In that case, will you tell me? Will you tell me why you hate the festival and Holly Ridge so much?"

I'm not sure if it was Blaire's scent overtaking the air, or the fact that I thought Blaire was already in a weakened state from all the bad news and wouldn't remember my story, but I decided to share.

"Twenty years ago, I went to the Holly Ridge festival for the first time by myself. I was hoping it would get me into the Christmas spirit. And when I showed up and took it all in, some boys from Holly Ridge recognized me in my Winterberry Glen Middle School sweatshirt, they threw some snowballs at me, and told me that people from Winterberry Glen don't deserve to enjoy the festival, and that I should go back to my side of the river. I was already losing faith in Christmas and miracles for a lot of other reasons, but that right then is when I decided Christmas wasn't for me anymore."

Blaire looked at me with something that looked unfortunately close to pity in her eyes, and I knew that sharing time was over and we needed to get out of the small space.

"Okay, well, I don't know about you, but I've got other things to do than hang out in this basement with old, bad memories all day. Let's get this cleaned up."

I stood up, leaning across Blaire's body to pick up a binder of newspapers at the same time she stood, leaning forward to unload the microfiche machine. Once again, I found myself touching Blaire's hair when I shouldn't be, but this time, my nose was buried in it. We both froze as I inhaled her honey scent once again. I felt myself drawing back, dragging my nose along her hairline. Okay, I'll admit it. I was nuzzling. I drew back even further, so I could see Blaire's eyes, her blue eyes speckled with grey in the dark lighting of the basement.

I'm not sure if I leaned forward or if Blaire rose on her tiptoes, but suddenly the distance between our mouths was gone and our lips met. Blaire's right hand came up to rest on my chest while my hand found its way to her waist, with the other rising to tangle in her hair.

At this contact, Blaire pulled her head back slightly and blinked slowly at me, licking her lips, but she didn't push me away. With determination in her eyes before, she tangled her left hand in the hair at the nape of my neck and eliminated any distance left between us, crashing her lips into mine. I felt all of Blaire's curves pressing against me. When I bit at her bottom lip, I received a gasp as a reward, and suddenly our tongues were tangling as well. I felt a groan leave my chest and wondered why we hadn't been kissing all along. Blaire tasted like honey and lemon and felt like I had kissed her a thousand times before.

Suddenly, the door slammed to the stairwell just beyond our

research room, and we jumped apart. Blaire touched her slightly swollen lips and realized where she was, who we were, and what we had just learned.

"I . . . I have to go," she stammered, lifting her bag off the floor, trying to push the door instead of pulling in her haste to put distance between us. Blaire didn't look back as she took off, leaving the door open behind her, and dashed up the stairs. I stood dumbfounded before I realized Mrs. Sanderson would have clocked her leaving by herself in a rush, and I did not want to be at the receiving end of that questioning. I quickly finished putting away all the film and binders Blaire had looked through and followed her path out of the library, all the while remembering what Blaire tasted like on my mouth.

Chapter 12.5

Blaire (11:18 p.m.): Okay, I know you're still up because that new monster romance novel came out today, so I'm breaking my no Cole after 11:00 p.m. talk rule. I have to tell you something.

Charlotte (11:19 p.m.): Putting away the blue aliens gladly. I feel like this is going to be juicy.

Blaire (11:21 p.m.): So you know how we went to the Winterberry Glen library today? Well, what we found out was just awful for Holly Ridge, and I was upset, and he told me a story about a formative moment in his childhood, and then... well, we kissed.

Charlotte (11:22 p.m.): IN THE LIBRARY? OH MY GOD, BLAIRE! That's been on your bucket list since you were fifteen. Thank goodness it wasn't with Chuckie Mancine. Have you SEEN the latest on his embezzling drama?

Blaire (11:23 p.m.): Uh, C? Focus, please?

Charlotte (11:25 p.m.): Right, of course, sorry. Okay, so you shared a moment and then a MOMENT. How was the kiss? What happened next?

Blaire (11:25 p.m.): The kiss was... everything fifteen-year-old Blaire didn't know to want because adult boys kiss so much better. But well then... I ran. *face palm emoji*

Charlotte (11:27 p.m.): Oh my god, you guys were made for each other. He ran first and now you've run away. Are you going to send him a meeting invitation series for virtual meetings now?

Blaire (11:29 p.m.): No! Definitely not. Then he'll know it meant something. But I am going to take a page out of his book and pretend it never happened. We know he won't bring it up, so that should be safe.

Charlotte (11:30 p.m.): So, it meant something, huh?

Blaire (11:31 p.m.): Nope. Nevermind. Definitely didn't mean that. The Cole-talk ban is back in place. Night, C!

Charlotte (11:32 p.m.): *Jennifer Lawrence Yeah, okay.gif*

Charlotte (11:32 p.m.): Goodnight, B.

Austin (9:05 a.m.): So, Cole, anything you want to tell me about your day yesterday?

Cole: (9:23 a.m.): I tried a new smoothie recipe for breakfast? It wasn't a hit.

Austin (9:25 a.m.): Of course it wasn't, because you insist on putting spinach in every single smoothie you make. You're setting yourself up for failure. But no, that's not what I was talking about.

Cole: (9:27 a.m.): Then nope, the day was pretty uneventful. Why do you ask?

Austin: (9:29 a.m.): You lying liar who lies. I know that you went into the library with Ms. Greene, but Ms. Greene left alone, looking flushed and in a hurry. And you left five minutes later, looking dazed and yet scowly all at the same time.

Cole: (9:31 a.m.): Who was your date last night? Mike from the auto body shop? Or did you finally get Missy from the dog groomers to agree to go out with you?

Austin: (9:33 a.m.): I never reveal my sources, but it may or may not have been someone who is employed at a business with a great view of the library's front door. Regardless. Did you do something dirty in the stacks?

Cole: (9:35 a.m.): What? No, we were in one of the research rooms with the microfiche machines.

Austin: (9:36 a.m.): But you DID do something dirty?!

Cole: (9:38 a.m.): I'm only telling you this because I know you'll be relentless. Fine. We may have kissed.

Austin: (9:39 a.m.): It's about damn time. I was starting to think your dick might explode before you ever touched her.

Cole: (9:41 a.m.): My dick's fine, thanks. And she might have kissed me? She definitely kissed me back.

Cole: (9:43 a.m.): I don't know, it all happened so fast. And then she ran away, so I'm not expecting any repeats. Which is for the best, because the state explicitly forbids a romantic relationship between us and I want this job.

Austin: (9:45 a.m.): She ran away this time? The irony. So, that bad at kissing, huh?

Cole: (9:53 a.m.): *middle finger emoji*

Austin: (9:55 a.m.) *laughing crying emoji*

Chapter 13

December 1

Blaire

December was finally here. In normal years, the festival would have opened last weekend, immediately following Thanksgiving. But, as I was only too aware, this was not a normal year. I was reeling from what happened at the Winterberry Glen library—both historical and present day. Sometime during my middle of the night musings, I realized there needed to *be* a Holly Ridge going forward for the town to try to make amends for its downright grinchy actions a century ago, so I was moving forward to rock the festival and save the town. I'd figure out the rest as we went along.

We still had another two weeks to go until the festival started, but I was officially dreaming in Christmas movie format—everyone wearing ugly sweaters, occasionally talking in rhyme and more Uncle Eddie's had driven their RVs to the town square to empty their shitters than I could count over the past several nights. That was when I was sleeping. Many nights, I was up until 1:00 or 2:00 a.m. going over checklists and making plans for the next day, so Cole had them in his inbox first thing when he woke up. Then it was up at 7:00 a.m. to workout—my patience while I waited for his response.

This morning dawned with a special kind of hell, though. Cole and I had to head to the state capital for a meeting with the state audit office. Why this had to happen two weeks before the festival started and not a month ago when the budget was finalized, I wasn't totally sure, but as I looked at my watch, I realized Cole would pull up at my parents' front door in five minutes, so it was time to stop with the visions of sugar plums and get moving.

Grabbing my business backpack—*yes, they're a thing*—I took one last look in the mirror to double check my appearance. I was wearing black boots that came to just below my knee and burgundy tights under a black dress that wouldn't wrinkle too terribly in the long car ride. I grabbed my hunter green blazer from the back of my door and made my way down the stairs. It was December, and I was planning a holiday festival after all. I thought my outfit should hold a subtle nod to the season.

My boots were heavy on the hardwood stairs as I headed down them and I knew it would announce my presence to anyone who happened to be on the lower-level of the house. Turning into the kitchen to fill up a travel mug with one more cup of coffee for the road, I found my dad and Gretchen sitting at the island, the twins and Mom nowhere to be found.

"Where are Grandma and H&H off to this morning?" I asked, reaching for my favorite festive tumbler and the coffee pot someone had kindly left half-full on the warmer. As I opened the fridge to grab my chocolate mocha almond milk creamer, it was Gretchen who answered.

"They're off at Jitters for some before school hot chocolate and coming up with ideas for presents Holland and Hollis can buy for everyone with the money they've saved from their allowances all year." Gretchen sat on a kitchen stool, looking perfect, as always. "I'm not sure how you can put that stuff into your coffee every day," she continued. "It just tastes so artificial and overly sweet to me."

Dad moved to grab the tumbler lid out of the drying rack and handed it to me with a small smile, knowing I got my sweet tooth from him.

"Are you all set for your meeting?" Dad asked in an attempt to change the subject and not let Gretchen's comment get to me, which he knew it would, no matter how innocent her intentions.

"I'm as ready as I can be, I think," I huffed out, uttering a big sigh as I paused to enjoy the aroma and warmth of my holiday coffee treat. "I just wish we could have had this meeting a month ago when Cole and I finished the budget."

Dad grimaced, as he always did when he needed to deliver news we didn't want to hear.

"I found out from one of my sources that the state office has been trying to go through the City Council to schedule this meeting with you for a while. They told the state office this date would work best for you."

"If they hate being city councillors so much, why don't they all just resign?!" I responded. Exasperated once again that the council had bungled something so terribly. "Arthur and Agatha were born in this town. Even if they went away to boarding school as young children, don't they have a little bit of pride in their hometown and where they're from?"

"I wonder if they want the town to be taken over, so they can be rid of the responsibilities without having to quit," Gretchen mused.

Dad nodded. "I'm starting to think that might be the case myself."

"Well, they can have as little pride or care for this town as they want. The best thing they ever did for this town was hiring Blaire to come home and run the festival. She's our best chance to keep the town charter and move things forward for Holly Ridge."

I stared at Gretchen, a little stunned that she would have this opinion of me but feeling a warming in my heart that had nothing to do with the coffee in my hand. Dad just smiled knowingly at me. He had always tried to tell me that Gretchen was proud of the work I was doing, even if it wasn't something she could see herself ever wanting to do.

"Thanks, sis," I said quietly. I was saved from having to come up with anything else to say by a honk from out front.

"Well, that must be my ride, right out of an early 2000s rom-com, honking from the street instead of coming to the door to meet my father," my voice full of irony at Cole's approach to letting me know he was here.

"We're heading back right after the meeting is over this afternoon. We won't be back in time for dinner, but I'll see you tonight," I said, resigned to spend a full December day in the presence of Cole Thomas.

"Keep an eye on the weather," Dad said as I walked toward the front door. "The weather folks say that the storm is going to hit overnight tonight, but my knee says it might start much earlier. Be safe on your trip back."

As used to Dad's knee's weather predictions as I was to Hallmark Christmas movies always ending in happy ever afters, I nodded and smiled, leaving the room with a wave to both him and Gretchen.

I stopped just inside the front door to double-check my bag for my phone, the documents and spreadsheets we'd need for the meeting, and my emergency peppermint chocolate stash. As my head was bent looking into my open bag, I heard Gretchen come up beside me.

"Are you going to be okay with all this time with Cole in the car?"

I looked up, totally startled by this question. I had spent so much time trying not to think about how we would be trapped in a car together for almost eight hours today. Had I said something out loud?

"Oh, that guy? I mean, he gets on my nerves, but I'm sure based on the need to keep his desk organized entirely in right angles that he's such a meticulous driver that he'll just keep silent with his hands at ten and two and not talk at all so he's not distracted from the road. I'll just review my presentation on the way up and listen to some holiday music playlists on my earbuds on the way back. Easy peasy."

Gretchen raised her eyebrow, a move I wish I could pull off half as well, telling me she didn't buy my nonchalance.

"You sure about that? You just get this look on your face sometimes when you talk about him. Like you're trying not to think about Mom's pumpkin pie when it comes out of the oven the day before Thanksgiving, because you know you won't be eating it until much, much later."

It was these kinds of observations that made Gretchen such a kick-ass lawyer. I decided to grab the olive branch she held out to me in the kitchen earlier and try something new: confiding in my older sister.

"We've had a couple of . . . moments over the past few months. We never talked about it afterward, but I've seen some new sides of him throughout this process. I don't know, obviously it's a terrible idea. He's from Winterberry Glen. He has a major impact on the future of our town. He could totally swoop in and try to take credit for my successes, and, of course, there's the whole any-type-of-personal-relationship-is-against-the-state's-parameters thing. This will be the longest time we've spent together, just the two of us, well, ever, so I'm a little anxious about it. I'm sure he hasn't given it a second thought though, so I'm going to try to not give it any more myself."

"I know I haven't been around you a ton while you've been an adult," Gretchen started, a very big-sisterly look on her face. "But if someone can inspire a conflict of the heart in you months after one or two *moments*, that's not something to overlook. The role he has in the festival oversight does make things a little messy, but him being from Winterberry Glen should really be a nonissue. That's part of the future I think you could be a driving force of, B, starting a path forward between our two towns."

For the second time in just a few moments, I was stunned into silence by my big sister. And then, for the second time this morning, I was saved from answering a question by Cole announcing his presence, this time with a knock on the front door that I could tell meant he was annoyed that I wasn't immediately responsive to his car honk minutes ago.

Gretchen's eyes lit up at the opportunity to catch a glimpse of Cole in person, and I rolled my eyes as I reached for the doorknob to open the door.

And suddenly, Cole Thomas was at my front door. I didn't miss the way his eyes took in my boots, moving up my body until those brown eyes locked on mine.

"Your blazer won't be enough for how cold it is out here. Don't forget a coat. Also, we're now behind schedule, so I hope that coffee cup doesn't mean you'll need extra stops on the way there."

And with that gruffly spoken non-greeting, Cole turned on his heel and headed back to his black Jeep, which he had left running on the curb to keep the heat going. He stopped on the passenger side, opened the door for me, hesitated for a moment like he wasn't sure if he should wait for me to get in, obviously thought better of it, and walked around the front of the car to the driver's side.

Gretchen handed me my coat, delighted at the interaction she witnessed. "Well, here's your coat, sis. You better get going. Your pumpkin pie seems antsy to get on the road."

I could feel my cheeks redden from her teasing, but for once, I could also see that it was good-natured.

"Bye, Gretch. I hope Mom is picking out the loudest, most annoying toys for the twins as we speak."

I could hear her laughing as I walked down the sidewalk toward the open car door, and as I looked back after folding myself into Cole's car and closing the door, just to be enveloped in his scent, I saw my dad had joined her at the open front door, a knowing smile on his face.

Chapter 14

Cole

We had been on the road for half of the four-hour trip to the state capitol and Blaire and I had only spoken a handful of words, but I had snuck sidelong glances at her legs in that dress and those boots at least a dozen times. I flexed my hand on the steering wheel and focused again on the road ahead of me, reminding myself I should be grateful Blaire was buried in her meeting-preparation documents.

I learned that underneath Blaire's love of brightly colored spreadsheets was a deeply analytical and organized mind that viewed festivals as the heartbeat of a small town's economy and a way to see into the soul of a community. It wasn't a passion I saw myself sharing any time soon, but I could see that she was great at what she did and there was a reason she had been so successful in all the towns she had worked in before.

I was cautious to keep more of my internal workings under wraps, especially after I had revealed so much of myself at the library, but there were times those blue eyes pierced me in a way that made me feel like she could see right through me. It was unnerving, but it was also just easier to pretend I was still as much of a mystery to her as I was the day we first met.

Suddenly, Blaire blew out a heavy breath of air.

"Okay, I can't look at these spreadsheets anymore. I've been over this information a million times in the past week. I'm not sure there's anything they can ask me I won't be ready for."

"I think you're right. Everything you've sent me is incredibly detailed and I think they're going to be pleased with the budgets, the presale numbers for some of the ticketed events, and how you've arrived at your projections for general attendance."

I chanced a glance her way and was rewarded with a gorgeous smile on her face, her appreciation for my compliment evident in her eyes.

"Thanks, Thomas. Though I do have to admit that the updates you want every week have helped shape the direction I took with the presentation. I figured since you speak money, I should follow your instincts, since I'm more likely to speak in customer satisfaction, number of twinkle lights, and cups of hot chocolate served."

"That's selling yourself short, Greene," I responded. "You had all of this information in your reports all along. I just helped you pull it out and group it together, but everything you track and plan for is integral to a successful festival as well."

Blaire turned away from me to watch the scenery pass by as we sped down the highway so I couldn't see her expression anymore, but her voice sounded pleased as she thanked me again.

I cleared my throat, nodding at a rest stop sign we were passing.

"Do you need a stop? Or are you all set for a little while longer?"

"Well, since you're offering, I could probably use a stop now. You may have had a point about that extra cup of coffee and us keeping to a schedule, though we're still set to arrive an hour and a half before our meeting, so I guess we have a decent cushion."

I pushed up on my turn signal to use the exit ramp to head to the rest stop.

"I have a meeting with the head of the state audit office forty-five minutes before our meeting. It's unrelated to the festival, but that's why I wanted to get there so early."

I knew that this truth would have to come out eventually, but I braced myself for Blaire to realize I had misled her.

"Is the meeting really unrelated to the festival?" Blaire looked at me speculatively as she opened the door to get out of the car at the rest stop.

"Yes, it is. I have an opportunity to take a job with the state office after the first of the year, and I just have a few questions about the contract. Since we were going to be there anyway, they suggested we just meet in person." I answered her question over the hood of the car, stretching after spending so much time tensed at the steering wheel and heading toward the door of the rest stop.

Blaire stopped midway through putting on her winter coat.

"You're leaving Winterberry Glen? To work for the state audit office?"

"It's looking likely," I responded as I stepped up to her and pulled her coat the rest of the way onto her shoulders. It really was cold out with the impending snow. I couldn't stop myself from trying to take care of her. She looked so surprised at the news. I felt like I should crack open my doors a bit for her—explain why this is the next step for me.

"I know you love Holly Ridge and always wanted to go back there, but I never intended to stay in Winterberry Glen for this long. It's . . . time to move on."

I shrugged, and realizing I was still holding the front of Blaire's coat, I let go and started walking toward the rest stop door.

Blaire fell in step beside me but was silent as we approached the building. I opened the door to let her in before me. "Meet you back here in a few minutes?"

Blaire nodded and headed off to the women's room while I headed toward the men's room. Had I imagined a bit of disappointment behind Blaire's surprise that I would leave my hometown? I must have. If she was successful in pulling off the festival, that meant I'd be out of her hair if I stayed, and we'd have no reason to stay in touch. Since the success of the festival and continued existence of her town was her end goal, she had to be hoping to be rid of me.

I didn't see Blaire when I exited the men's room, so I headed to the convenience store and grabbed a bottle of water for me and a Diet Coke for Blaire. At the last second, I grabbed the trail mix I noticed Blaire eating at several of our meetings. As I headed back toward the parking lot, I saw Blaire standing outside in her coat and what I had to admit was an adorable pom beanie, staring up at the sky, which had started to emit light flurries of snowflakes.

"Trying to catch a snowflake on your tongue?"

Blaire started, obviously not hearing me approach her from behind. I noticed a few snowflakes caught on her eyelashes and in the hair framing her face, and I found myself wanting to brush them away, just as an excuse to touch her again.

"No," she smiled indulgently at me. "Just looking at the clouds, trying to figure out if these are just flurries or the start of that storm that's headed our way."

"All the weather reports say the storm is starting overnight tonight, so we should be back home before anything gets too bad."

"Whatever you say, Thomas. Shall we get back on the road, so you can make your meeting?" Blaire responded, the smug look on her face not matching her response, turning to head back toward the car.

I guess Blaire had processed my news about the job and wasn't impressed with my intentions of taking it, but was deciding to let the issue drop. I tried to keep my emotions tamped down, knowing we still had lots of one-on-one time left today. Why did I care what she thought about my future plans, anyway? Why did I want her to be more openly disappointed that I was leaving, or at least offer her opinion on the whole thing? It's not like she's ever kept her opinion to herself before this.

I started the car and turned on the radio for the first time on the trip. I focused on getting us out of the parking lot and merged back onto the highway. After a little while, I heard Blaire snicker from the passenger seat.

"What?"

"Oh, nothing."

"Blaire. What?"

"I was right that you're a ten-and-two driver, but I thought the radio would stay off the entire time. But now, I'm realizing it's tuned to NPR, which is basically the station equivalent of silence, so I guess I wasn't too far off."

"Let me guess," I responded, feeling my mood lift now that we were returning to our familiar sparring instead of her brooding silence. "If you were driving, we would still be in the middle of an epic holiday music playlist you had curated just for this trip?"

"It's after Thanksgiving! It's socially acceptable for me to listen to my holiday music playlists around other people now!" Blaire responded, seeming to revel in our back and forth as much as I was.

I shook my head.

"Seasonal music hasn't really been my thing for a long time. I have an investing podcast, or a new episode of my favorite true crime podcast lined up, if you'd like to listen to that instead."

"Cole Thomas, a true crime podcast fan? That does surprise me," Blaire teased.

"I like to try to figure things out, especially if there's a money trail to follow."

"That's a little less surprising," Blaire responded as she navigated to my podcasts on the car's display screen.

"I think I saw online that all the episodes this month feature cases that have some sort of holiday tie-in," I admit just as she presses play and the first ad selling us on a bed and breakfast in the area started playing.

"Not quite the uplifting holiday message I usually go for, but you're finally speaking my language, Thomas."

Blaire settled into her seat, her eyes on the road ahead of us as she listened to the hosts set up the background of the crime and I felt my hands slip slightly from their ten-and-two positions as I allowed myself to, just for a brief second, revel in the feeling of rightness between Blaire and me.

Chapter 15

Blaire

I spent the forty-five minutes Cole was in his meeting alternating between getting more and more nervous about my meeting, wondering if Cole was being completely truthful about the nature of his meeting, and ignoring the feeling that opened up in my stomach when I thought about Cole leaving Winterberry Glen. Then there was the idea that Gretchen put in my head that it didn't matter where Cole was from if he was invading my thoughts so deeply and regularly. Turning over what that could mean for the future of my relationship with Cole had plagued me the entire time I was pretending to look at my spreadsheets—honestly, I had those things memorized a week ago. I had needed to give up the ruse that I was looking at them and make Cole engage with me so that I didn't try to convince him to pull over and kiss me again. Cole's revelation about his position with the state audit office connected some dots about why he accepted the assignment to oversee the festival financial process when he was so disdainful of Holly Ridge and the holidays all together. And I took some relief in knowing he had a contract already, which meant that the job wasn't dependent on the outcome of the festival. I could deal with Cole's disdain for Holly Ridge, that was something he was born with, but I didn't know how I would feel if he was actively rooting for me to fail so he could move up in the government finance world. But it also caused me to rearrange— yet again—my changing feelings around Cole Thomas. Cole seemed a bit hurt I wasn't expressing more emotions about his news, but once we recovered our equilibrium and started teasing each other again, something settled inside me.

All too soon for my liking, someone from the audit office came down the hallway to walk me back to the windowless conference room they had reserved for us for the afternoon and had been meeting with Cole. The energy in the room when I entered was congenial. I looked at Cole to see if I could read on his face how the meeting went, but his expression gave nothing away. I settled into the seat next to him, passed around a packet of handouts, and reached under the table to wipe my sweaty palms on my skirt. I felt a quick, but firm squeeze on my wrist, and hopefully managed to hide my surprise that Cole would risk such a move of familiarity in front of his future bosses. Assuming his intention was to steady and calm me, it worked, and I launched into the presentation I had prepared.

After all the worry, nerves and preparation, our meeting with the state audit office passed by in a blur of numbers, statistics, serious looks, and head nods. Cole continued to be a comforting presence next to me, even though most of the questions from the officials were directed at me. Cole offered his support and endorsement of my budget and confirmed I had been following all the rules the state audit office had set out. His endorsement seemed to finally relax the committee, which grated on me, because why should his assurance be worth more than mine, the one who had built the charts and tables they were examining? That wasn't Cole's fault, though. He was simply answering a question as asked, and I appreciated his earnest support.

Next thing I knew, we were shaking hands with the state officials, receiving their seemingly genuine well wishes on the festival's success, and walking back to the parking garage. We were met with a completely different scene from the one we had left behind when we entered the office building two hours earlier—everything was blanketed with a covering of white.

"Guess we have an answer to that flurry or snowstorm question," I said to Cole as I carefully made my way down the slick marble steps as he did the same right behind me.

Once we were back on solid, yet snow-covered ground, I looked over at Cole and saw his brow furrowed as he scrolled through the forecast and traffic reports on his phone.

"It's moving across the state toward home. The interstates seem to still be fairly clear. We may be able to get ahead of the worst of it if we hit the road now."

Considering we were both northeastern born and raised, driving in snow was something we were taught when we learned to drive and I trusted Cole and his all-wheel drive to keep us safe as we tried to make it home, so I easily agreed to his plan. I had images of a celebratory dinner in the city after our meetings, but that would be too much like the Pepper's setting last summer, so it was probably best we hit the road and grabbed food when we inevitably needed to stop for fuel or a bathroom break.

We got on the road and resumed listening to Cole's true crime podcast. I couldn't keep the smile off my face as I thought about how he brought up that they were holiday themed, knowing this was a bridge of our listening tastes. I recognized they may be episodes Cole would have skipped if it wasn't for this time we were sharing in the car today.

The snow continued to fall, the sky continued to darken, and I noticed the crease in Cole's forehead deepened as his focus increased on the road. I stopped making comments on the podcast when I realized he wasn't really listening anymore, giving all his attention to the slowing traffic and slushy roads around us.

Suddenly, the vehicles in front of us came to an abrupt stop and Cole slammed on the brakes to avoid ending up in the trunk of the car directly ahead of us.

"Fuck!" he yelled, his arm coming across my chest like an extra restraint, even though I was buckled in. Just as instinctively, my hands wrapped around his forearm, gripping tight. The car fishtailed slightly due to the harsh braking, but Cole was able to regain control of the car with no harm to us or anyone around us.

Both of us were breathing heavily after the sudden adrenaline burst. We made eye contact across the middle console and his eyes moved all around my face, trying to take in my emotions.

"Are you all right?" Cole asked.

"Yes, I'm fine. You?"

"Yes. That was a little too close for comfort. Thank goodness for snow tires."

Through all this checking in, I was aware that his arm was still across my breasts, his hand curling protectively around my right shoulder, and my hands were still on his arm, though my grip had loosened. There was nothing sexual about the protective intent of the motion, but as our breathing slowed, our eye contact remained steady. I was aware of the strength of his arm, and how the weight of just this one limb felt pressing down on me. I thought I saw his eyes darken, but it could have been a trick of the last of the daylight leaving the sky, leaving us in a sea of red brake lights and illuminated sparkling white flakes.

I took a deep breath, moving his arm with the rise and fall of my chest and released his forearm. Cole released his grip as well, retracting his arm by tracing the back of his hand along my collarbone. My breath hitched at the tender touch, which seemed to break his reverie, and focused on the matter at hand—that we were on an expressway that was starting to crawl forward again after moments at a complete stop, in a snowstorm, in the now dark night.

"Did you happen to notice the last exit we passed?" Cole asked, his voice a bit deeper than normal.

"I didn't. Let me grab my phone and check."

I leaned down to fish my phone out of my bag, happy to have something to do with my hands, so I didn't grab his arm and put it back where it had been moments earlier. That had to be the adrenaline talking, right? Who had this sort of reaction to a near-accident situation?

"It looks like we just passed exit 73."

"Okay, so we have another 120 miles before we get to the exit for home. The roads are only going to get worse, so I think we might need to find somewhere to stay for the night."

Cole was right in this logic, but my stomach twisted at the thought of staying in the same place as Cole overnight.

"Can you look up hotels or anywhere nearby that might have two rooms available?" Cole continued.

Right, two rooms, of course. Because, obviously, two work colleagues who hated each other would stay separately. My stomach unknotted, and I batted away the disappointment that threatened to seep in along with the relief of having that anxiety resolved.

As Cole focused on crawling us forward, I called everything at the next several exits, and everyone was full. I was told there was "No Room at the Inn" more than once, and experienced a taste of Christmas exasperation that Cole seemed to be so familiar with.

I finally hit some luck with The Old Coach Inn, the proprietor letting us know that they absolutely had space for us and to come on over, they would keep some dinner warm for us too.

"Okay, Cole, we're heading to The Old Coach Inn, it's at the next exit which is exit—"

"69," he finished for me.

I snorted, the stress and length of the day finally catching up with me. Cole chuckled as well.

"What are you, a fourteen-year-old boy?"

"Maybe when I've been in a car for an hour and traveled three miles, it sends me to that mindset, Thomas. Okay?!"

Cole laughed softly at me, and then we were on the exit ramp, and I directed him to the bed and breakfast's parking lot, taking the last spot that someone had plowed out, though it was a losing battle, the falling snow refilling the parking spot and coming up to the bottom rim of the tires already.

I couldn't help my squeal as we got out of the car. Now that we were off the road and had secured a place to stay, I was able to focus on how beautiful the snow was and what a perfect Christmas scene the B&B portrayed in it. It had snow-covered eaves that were illuminated by strands of white lights, the porch railings were draped with garland, a candle illuminated each window, and wreaths hung on the front doors. If we had to be stranded for the night, at least it was somewhere they did Christmas right.

"Good grief," Cole muttered as we opened the front door, and more of the same level of festive decorations were displayed in the interior.

"Shhh!" I shushed Cole, not wanting to hurt the feelings of the kind-looking woman at the desk, who had looked up as soon as she heard the door open.

"Hi there!" the woman called as we approached the desk. "You must be my last stranded travelers! I'm Louise, and welcome to The Old Coach Inn."

"Hi Louise. I'm Blaire and this is Cole. Thanks so much for holding rooms for us. Everywhere else we tried was full, and it was time to get off the road, get warm, and wait for the snow to stop."

Louise's expression morphed into one of concern.

"Oh dear. Rooms? No, I'm afraid we just have one room left. It does have a king-sized bed in it. I heard you say you need a room for two people, not that you needed two rooms. Everything else is full, either with people already staying with us, or folks like your-selves, who needed to get off the road and rest their heads for the night."

"Is there a couch in the room, Louise? Or maybe a cot we could have brought up into the room?" Cole chimed in at this point.

"I'm afraid not. It's a cozy little room. There isn't space for much besides the bed, nightstands, and armoire. It does have its own bathroom, though!" Louise answered brightly, either immune to grumpy travelers or choosing to ignore Cole's look of displeasure at the lack of sleeping options.

I jumped back in before Cole could say anything to lose us this room for the night.

"Thank you so much Louise. We understand there are a lot of people who need a place to stay on a night like tonight. We'll figure it out."

There was a bathroom. He could sleep in the bathtub for all I cared.

"On another note, do you happen to have any extra toiletries or some lost and found clothes we could raid? We weren't planning being out overnight, obviously, and it would be a bit uncomfortable to sleep in this." I swept my hands at my business attire, not at all conducive for sleeping.

"I have some toothbrushes here and there are typical toiletries in the room, but our lost and found has been thoroughly raided already."

Louise started to ring her hands as she delivered this news, apparently not as immune to Cole's glower as I had originally estimated.

"Okay! I mean, a dress is basically a nightgown, right?"

"I have my gym bag that I got out of the back of my Jeep. I have a few things here. We'll make it work."

"When did you get that?"

"When you were gazing at the Christmas card scene like you just stepped into a snow globe, Greene."

I refused to be ashamed of my love of all things Christmas, so I just raised my eyebrow at Cole, knowing my arch wasn't as good as Gretchen's but would still get my message across.

"I'm so glad you love the decorations, dear! The inn has been in my family for generations and we always love decorating for the holidays. It's a guest activity the weekend after Thanksgiving."

I tore my gaze away from Cole's and smiled at Louise.

"The house looks absolutely beautiful. I'm planning the Christmas festival in Holly Ridge, so I consider myself something of an expert in decorating touches and I can tell you have an excellent eye."

At this, any harm that was caused by Cole's glower was rectified and Louise flushed with pleasure.

"Well, thank you, my dear. Let me go grab your dinners out of the warmer in the kitchen. I'll be right back."

Louise walked away and I looked back at Cole, who was avoiding my eyes by looking at his phone again.

"My battery is almost dead and all I have is a car charger. Guess I'll just be unreachable until tomorrow."

Cole said this with a frown, his finger flying across the screen, apparently trying to send out one last missive before his phone powered down. I had a battery pack in my bag, but after his crack about my Christmas decoration gazing, I wasn't feeling particularly charitable.

Louise was back with two to-go containers full of food that smelled delicious and a bottle of red wine to go with it.

"To make up for the mix-up with the rooms and all," Louise said with a smile, handing the food and wine to Cole and then handing me a key with the number six on the tag attached to it.

"Y'all are the room at the end of the hall on the third floor. You'll have the best view of the snowstorm . . . well, you'll see. Have a great night. Breakfast is served starting at 7:00 a.m.!"

Having been dismissed, we made our way up two flights of stairs and to room number six. I opened the door and held it so Cole could make his way into the room.

The room was a complete dream, and I felt like it was going to be wasted on Cole and me sharing it together. The bed faced a three-paneled massive window which offered, as promised, a beautiful view of the grounds the B&B was housed on. More strings of lights were strung on trees throughout the immediate property, which illuminated the area and painted a beautiful winter wonderland.

I walked toward the window and took in the scene for a little bit while Cole set things down behind me. I heard him unzipping his bag and rustling around but couldn't be bothered to check and see what he was doing. I couldn't take my eyes off the view.

"C'mon, Thomas, holiday-related things removed, you have to admit that's a gorgeous winter view."

I heard Cole approaching from where he had been by the bed and came to stand next to me at the window. I looked over at him to find him not looking at the scene but watching me as I gazed out the window. He opened and closed his mouth a few times before saying, "It's hard to see how pretty it is when it's stopping us from getting home, but yeah, I guess it's not horrible."

I rolled my eyes at his inability to live in the moment and turned around to locate dinner, or more importantly that bottle of wine.

"Um, if you want to change before we eat, I have a T-shirt and gym shorts here that you can wear if you'd like," Cole said awkwardly.

"Oh. Okay? I mean, I don't want to take them from you. You're the one who had a bag in the car."

"It's okay, I have an undershirt on under my button-down, and there were a pair of sweatpants in the bag as well, so we'll both be more comfortable that way. Do you want to change out here or in the bathroom?"

"I'll head into the bathroom," I answered, needing to splash some cold water on my face and game up for the fact that Cole and I would be in the same room, presumably in the same bed, All. Night. Long.

Before heading into the bathroom, I stopped to unzip and take off my boots. I groaned slightly in relief when my legs were freed from the boots, looking up to catch Cole watching me out of the corner of his eye. I had thought I was imagining his eyes straying to my boots a few times throughout the day, but this was the first time I had actually caught him in the act. The sidelong glance told me I wasn't the only one feeling the tension between us. Yup, definitely was going to need some cold water and game face to make it through this night.

I went into the bathroom and closed the door, leaning back against it, looking at my flushed face in the mirror. This was fine. It was a king-sized bed. I bet Cole slept like a vampire on his back with his arms crossed and didn't move all night. We could make a pillow wall, all would be great. I went ahead and splashed water on my face, twisted my hair up into a messy bun on top of my head, and changed out of my clothes and into the clothes Cole had set aside for me. I had to roll the shorts a few times so they didn't fall below my knees, and decided the shirt was baggy enough to remove my bra without detection.

As I opened the door to re-enter the bedroom, I realized I was going to spend the night enveloped in Cole's scent and had to stop myself from tucking my nose under the collar of his T-shirt and breathing deep. I stepped back into the room and saw Cole illuminated by the lights from the window, apparently deciding to give the winter wonderland a second chance. His undershirt clung to his defined upper body and was fitted to highlight his narrow waist, which drew my attention to the grey sweatpants that hung low on his hips. The hips where his hands were currently resting, drawing my eyes to that level like a beacon, noticing that those pants weren't *not* doing his ass a favor. He turned around suddenly when he heard me enter the room, and my eyes stayed at hip level and I was now taking in his grey sweat-panted crotch. My eyes briefly met his, which told me he had caught me in my crotch gazing, and then my eyes were dancing around the room, trying to locate that bottle.

Cold water and a game face were not going to be enough. It was time for wine.

Chapter 16

Cole

Cole (9:07 p.m.): Hey Austin, I'm going to be stranded off the interstate tonight. The storm hit faster and harder than expected. My phone is going to die until we get back into the car in the morning. Can you go check on Mom first thing and shovel her sidewalk if the snow has stopped?

Austin (9:32 p.m.): You got it, man. Sorry to hear you're stuck overnight.

Austin (9:33 p.m.) And without your phone, whatever will you do? *devil emoji*

Cole (9:33 p.m.): Thank you, that's a huge relief. I owe you one.

Cole (9:34 p.m.): Blaire has hers, so we can set an alarm and be aware of any emergency alerts or anything. It'll be fine.

Austin (9:35 p.m.): Wait, wait, wait. Blaire's phone is in range where you can hear it? Does that mean you're in the same room? Is the storm not the only thing getting hit fast and hard?

Cole (9:36 p.m.): Phone's dying, and also, you're dead to me. Thanks again. Night.

Austin (9:37 p.m.): *Laughing Emoji* *Eggplant Emoji* *Laughing Emoji*. Night bro. Don't do anything I wouldn't do.

At that point, my phone finally did die. I was relieved to know that Austin would be over at Mom's house first thing in the morning so she didn't try to walk outside before things had been shoveled, or worse, try to take care of it herself. I knew he would follow through, even if he was less than supportive of my current predicament. I was glad my phone had died. I didn't need Austin texting every few moments, asking something that would surely scar Blaire for life if she caught a glimpse of it.

That brought my mind back to the beautiful woman who was currently changing into my clothes in the bathroom of our shared room for the night. I made quick work of unbuttoning my button-down and exchanging my dress pants for my sweatpants. At least it didn't seem like she was going to shower before changing. I don't think I could handle it if Blaire was naked, wet, *and* in my clothes. My sweatpants surely wouldn't hide the reaction that would bring out in me. I stared out the window and let myself get hypnotized by the falling snow to calm the hardening that errant train of thought had begun.

Suddenly I heard the door open behind me, and I took a deep breath, steeling myself to see Blaire in my clothes. I turned around, only to catch Blaire's eyes darting up from the very sweatpants that were more and more guaranteed to make a fool of me with every passing moment. Her eyes danced around the room, finally landing on the side table where I had set the to-go boxes and bottle of wine and started toward it. Blaire ignored the food and went right for the wine.

"At least it's a twist off, but it looks like there are no cups in the room. Out of the bottle okay with you?"

Put my mouth where Blaire's mouth had been? Sure thing, not a problem.

"Yup," I answered. "Though we should eat too. I don't know about you, but I'm starving."

"Okay. Fine, Dad." Blaire blushed red when she realized what she'd said. I certainly heard it and reeled my mind back from other scenarios where Blaire might call me daddy. It was definitely time for some wine.

Blaire plopped herself down on the floor at the foot of the bed, bottle of wine in hand, resting her back against the bottom of the bed frame. This allowed her to face the window and the snow that continued to fall at a steady pace. I settled in next to her, bringing the food containers with me, thankful that Louise had provided some cutlery, even if she forgot about glasses for the wine. I passed one of the containers to Blaire, who set the bottle of wine down between us and flipped open the lid to her container.

"What have we got?" I asked unnecessarily, as I opened my container. I felt the need to fill the silence at this particular moment.

"Looks like some tortellini. Mmm, how perfect for a cold night. I wonder if it's homemade."

Blaire dug in, moaning as she savored the first bite.

I quickly dug in myself, trying to ignore the sounds of food-related pleasure occurring next to me. Much like her "dad" comment, it took my mind to a place where I imagined other ways I could make Blaire moan, and how it would feel to be responsible for that kind of pleasure.

"It definitely tastes homemade. It tastes a lot like some my mom used to make before . . ." I trailed off, realizing I was about to address a part of my life I usually didn't talk about with people other than Austin.

"Before what?" Blaire asked curiously, taking a break from her dinner to take a sip of wine.

Transfixed by the sight of the bottle at her lips, I answered without realizing.

"Before my dad left. My mom sort of stopped cooking, at least a lot of super involved homemade dishes, after that."

"Oh."

Blaire handed me the bottle of wine, which I gladly accepted and proceeded to take a few swallows.

"That sounds like it was a really hard time for both of you," her eyes full of the type of empathy that came from a person who had a wealth of feelings and emotions to lend to those around her, but also came from a healthy family home and couldn't personally imagine what something like that would be like.

"It was," I admitted, putting the wine back on the ground and dragging my fork through the pasta, suddenly not very hungry anymore.

"Things were better in some ways, because they weren't fighting anymore and we weren't walking on eggshells around Dad, but at the same time, Mom was just really, really sad that he was gone and we were alone. It was hard for me to understand because my dad and I never got along, but she really loved him and when he left, a light sort of went out inside her. It's one reason I stayed close to Winterberry Glen all these years and took the job with the Glen's government. It meant I wouldn't have to leave her too."

Blaire reached out to put her hand on my arm in a comforting sort of gesture and I glanced at the bottle, wondering just how much wine we had drunk that had me opening up this way. But I realized it was just her. She made me feel like I could share myself with her in a way that I hadn't done with very many people. I think I had subconsciously realized this about Blaire, and that made me feel like I needed to reinforce my walls around her.

"How does she feel about the potential of you leaving Winterberry Glen and moving to the state capital?" Blaire asked, proving that her analytical mind didn't miss much.

"She doesn't know yet. I didn't want to bring it up until I knew it was a sure thing, and that the contract was going to be one that would allow me to set up some things for her I won't be able to do since I won't be around regularly. She started seeing a therapist a few years ago and I think that really has helped her. She's made a few comments here and there that make me think she knows I'm ready to move on, but it'll be a hard conversation to have."

Blaire nodded at that, picking at the label on the wine bottle.

"I wasn't quite ready to come home to work on the festival when the council called. Of course, planning my hometown festival was the dream, but I wanted to be sure that when I got the job, it wasn't going to be because of who my dad was to the town, but because of my record with event planning and small-town festivals. And then the council called, getting me into this situation, because they knew if they sold it just right, about the Greene legacy of coming through for Holly Ridge, I wouldn't be able to turn it down."

I winced, remembering the shot I took at her about her dad the first day we met. I frowned further, remembering that had sparked her to make a comment about my dad in return. Neither of us knew how deep those comments would cut the other at the time, but we certainly took aim and hit each other's weak spots on the first try.

We sat in an easy silence now, passing the bottle of wine back and forth, food containers discarded to the side. Our shoulders rested so they were just touching, and I could smell Blaire's shampoo from this angle. It took effort to keep my eyes trained on the winter scene outside, and to not turn to gaze at the gorgeous scene taking place in our room—this intelligent, kind, and lovely woman sitting next to me, flushed from the red wine and wearing my clothes.

"I think it's probably time we went to bed," I finally said, needing to burst the bubble of comfortable intimacy we had accidentally created. "Maybe there are some extra blankets in the armoire I can make a bed here on the ground with—"

"No way," Blaire started. "You got us through that storm safely, and tomorrow probably isn't going to be super easy, either. You need a good night's sleep. I should offer to sleep on the floor too, but I'm not that gracious when I set my sights on a cushy king-sized bed like this one. It's a huge bed. You'll stay on your side, and I'll stay on mine."

"Okay. It should be fine."

I wasn't sure if I was agreeing with her or trying to convince myself this was the truth.

I headed to the bathroom to brush my teeth, chug a few glasses of water to counteract the wine's effects tomorrow morning, and have a private conversation with my cock that it needed to not get any ideas about funny business.

I came out of the bathroom to Blaire bent over the bed, ass in the air, making a dividing line in the middle of the bed with the bolster pillow. It would only come down to my stomach when I laid down, but if it made her feel more comfortable, I wasn't going to argue with her.

"Seemed to be a better idea than just throwing it on the floor?" Blaire said, phrasing it more like a question than a sure statement.

"Smart thinking."

"Okay, I'm just going to go brush my teeth and wash my face now."

When Blaire exited the bathroom a few minutes later, she did a sort of stutter step as she took me in, lying in the same bed she was about to crawl into. Taking a deep breath, she tucked her hair behind her ears, and wearing a face I was more familiar with when she had to face a reporter or the public, Blaire pulled back her side of the covers and slipped into bed.

"Goodnight, Cole," she said quietly as she turned off the last light in the room, plunging the room into darkness, save for the glow of the lights reflecting off the snow outside.

"Goodnight, Blaire," I responded, aware of every movement and breath she took as she settled in for the night. We laid in silence for a long while, both trying to stay still and control our breathing, until I finally heard her breathing even out, signaling to me she had fallen asleep. Then, and only then, did I let myself close my eyes and join her in the oblivion of sleep.

Chapter 17

Blaire

I was so warm and cozy in front of this fireplace, the warmth from the flames flickering and licking my skin with a heat that was close to being too warm. This was a much more relaxing scene than the festival anxiety dreams I had been having. My back was up against something firm, perhaps the bottom of a couch? A comforting white noise whirred in the background as I snuggled deeper into my blankets, inhaling a comforting and clean scent that was so familiar. Mmm, Cole; I could be wrapped up in his scent for hours. I smiled and sighed, pushing back against the couch, when suddenly the couch grumbled and I felt the blankets tighten around my hips.

Shit!

My eyes popped open, and my entire body stiffened. I was snuggled up to Cole's firm chest, hearing his steady breaths in my ear where his face was nestled in my neck. Our legs were tangled together, and I realized I needed to be very careful about extricating myself to deal with the full bladder that was suddenly making itself present.

As my feet hit the floor, I squeaked at the cold on my feet and then slapped my hands over my mouth, looking over my shoulder at Cole, still sleeping, illuminated by nothing more than the reflection off the snow. I realized the twinkle lights out on the grounds were off, and I noticed as I tiptoed toward the bathroom that the room seemed much colder now than it had been when we fell asleep a few hours ago.

Did the power go out? I wondered and tested the light switch once I was inside the bathroom with the door closed. Nothing happened when I flicked the switch.

Well shit, there goes that hot breakfast I was hoping for in the morning, I grumbled to myself silently, finishing up with my late-night business and washing my hands with cold water before heading back into the bedroom. I knew with the power out, the best thing to do was get back into bed, but our bolster divider was long gone, and as I gazed at Cole lying there on his back and looking younger and less stressed than I had ever seen him, it felt like I was entering a very dangerous swimming hole. A swimming hole that looked so inviting, yet also threatened to overtake me if I dipped my toe in.

At that point, Cole stirred and noticed me standing there next to the bed.

"Hey," he said, his voice thick and low with sleep, "is everything okay?"

"Yeah, just needed to use the bathroom. The power's out though."

"Oof, that's rough in this cold, but I'm not surprised with the amount of snow we got. I guess you better get back under the covers quickly, get warmed up."

Cole probably meant this for my general well-being, but it felt like an invitation straight to the center of me, causing my nipples to tighten and my core to clench as I gazed at him. He looked so fucking handsome, lying in a bed in the most charmingly Christmassy bed and breakfast from my romance-fueled dreams.

I nodded and gingerly got back into the bed, drawing the blankets up to my chin to hide those traitorous nipples, turning so my back was to Cole. Maybe this way the rest of me wouldn't get any ideas to follow the path certain parts of my body were very interested in pursuing.

Cole reached out from his side of the bed to rub my arm over the top of the covers. "It's that cold out there?" he asked as he tried to warm me up by shoulder friction alone.

"It's mostly my feet from the cold floors. I can't feel warm while they're still so frigid."

"Well, bring them over here. I won't be able to get back to sleep with you shaking the bed like this. Body heat is Survival 101."

I wanted to turn around to see if there was any heat in his eyes as he suggested this like a good Boy Scout, but I didn't think I had the nerve. I scooted back to tangle my feet with his legs at the same time he scooted forward, and my brain registered that my feet were entangled in gloriously warm, but also very bare legs.

"Fuck, Cole. What happened to your sweatpants?!"

I tried to put distance between us, but Cole's arm reached out to band across my middle and keep me in place.

"They were going to be too bulky to sleep well in, so I thought I could be sneaky and go without them. I didn't count on you shoving down the pillow wall and being a contender for little spoon of the tristate area in the middle of the night."

I felt my cheeks warm, realizing that he had at some point woken up to us spooning, and had decided to not do anything to change our positions. Those dangerous thoughts were back again, warming me from the inside, and this time I arched my ass backward into Cole, being rewarded with a sharp intake of breath from the man in question and a promising bulge forming in his briefs.

"I didn't expect any contact quite like that either when I decided to lose the pants," Cole quipped, the husky and low quality returning to his voice, but presumably not from sleep this time.

We lay connected at my shoulders and his chest, my ass and

his groin, and my feet and his shins. Slowly, we melted together so I couldn't pick out any points where we weren't touching.

"You know, Boy Scout, more body heat would come from skin-to-skin contact," I ventured, the darkness of the night, the seclusion of the snowstorm, and that firm bulge poking me from behind, making me bold.

"You might have a point there," Cole agreed after a brief pause. At this his hand started to move upward from its starting point at my hips, taking my—well, actually his, shirt with it.

"Is this okay, Blaire?" he asked just before his hand and the hem of the shirt reached the bottom of my breast. Not trusting myself to *not* stop his path if I engaged my brain to speak, I answered by arching further so his hand was cupping my right breast, his fingers instinctually finding that hardened bud, gently caressing and tweaking it until I couldn't believe I considered my nipple hard before. A moan escaped my mouth before I could bite it back and I found myself rolling onto my back to give him access to its twin as well.

This put in me in a position to turn my head and face him for the first time since climbing back into this bed. Wanting to look at his face to see if it would betray any of his thoughts, I opened my eyes and turned to see his lips parted. His darkened eyes met mine, immediately betraying heat, wanting, and something that maybe looked a little like fear as well.

Wondering what my eyes were telling him, I closed them and tilted my face up to meet his lips for the first time since the research room, but it felt like we had been doing this all along. His lips knew how to move against mine instinctually, pouring his wanting and desire into me through this connection, his tongue moving against the seam of my lips. I parted them immediately to grant him access. The hand that wasn't under my shirt tangled into my hair, and my fingers found themselves clawing into his shoulder and scalp, needing to feel closer.

That need wasn't quite satisfied, so I straddled his firm and sturdy body, one leg on either side of his hips, leaning over his chest to not break our kisses, placing that bulge right where we both wanted it. This dislodged his hand from its ministrations under my shirt, so I sat up to whip it off, throwing it who knows where behind me. Cole lay beneath me, blinking up and looking slightly stunned.

"You're beautiful," he breathed out, sitting up to tug his shirt over his head in that sexy, effortless, two-hands-behind-the-head way all men seem to know how to do. Once we were both shirtless, he wrapped his arms around me. We met skin to skin for the first time, but were no longer aware of the chill in the room that had started us down this path. Our mouths met again, and I realized Cole had been holding back on me. Underneath that buttoned up exterior there was a courteous, but wild man waiting to be unleashed. One hand moved back to my hair, tilting and angling my head just the way he wanted it, demanding access to my mouth with his tongue.

I needed to move, so I rolled my hips to deepen the contact between his boxer-brief-covered cock and my gym-short-covered pussy. I was rewarded with a groan that originated deep in Cole's chest, but this time, no one ran to safety. Instead, Cole moved his mouth down my chin, back up to bite softly on my ear, and then he ran kisses down the side of my neck.

"Blaire, I never imagined . . . okay, well I have imagined, but I never dreamed this would happen tonight, so I don't have anything. You know, any protection. I don't suppose your all-prepared Blaire bag contains some condoms?" Cole asked me from his position against my neck, his fingers tracing circles around my lower back and hips.

"It definitely will going forward, but no, there's never been a need for them on the job before."

"Never?" Cole asked incredulously, lifting his head to meet my eyes, wide in shock.

I laughed.

"Thomas, I just straddled you and took my own shirt off.

Does that really scream shy virgin to you? I just meant work and . . . this . . . have never collided unexpectedly before."

"Got it. Caveman instincts retracted," Cole replied, rolling his eyes at himself for once.

I took this opportunity to lavish some kisses and attention of my own to Cole's neck, biting a little less gently on his ear, blowing hot air after to ease the sting and being rewarded with an unintentional jerk of his hips.

"No protection takes some things off the table, but I still am going to need to do some exploring," I said as I pushed him back to a flat position on the bed, scooting myself back so that I could pull the waistband of his briefs down to reveal the Goldilocks of cocks Cole had been keeping there all this time. Not too long, not too short, just thick enough.

Oh, I can't wait to feel that inside me next time, I thought to myself as I ran a curled hand up and down the firm shaft in front of me. *Next time! Nope, don't go there, Blaire. Just focus on the here and now.*

"Next time . . ." Cole started, apparently having the same wandering thoughts as me, but just not quite as in control of not voicing those thoughts as I was. I couldn't go there, so I silenced him by taking the head of his cock into my mouth, and from there neither of us thought about much except what was happening in this room on this winter night. I focused on the feel of his heavy rod in my mouth, the manly and slightly salty taste coating my tongue.

I quickly found a rhythm, taking him a little deeper in the back of my throat every time. Cole's breathing picked up and occasionally a quiet groan or moan escaped him, letting me get a glimpse of an uncontrolled Cole Thomas, and boy, did I like it. Giving my jaw a break, I worked the shaft covered in saliva firmly with one hand and took his balls in the other.

"Blaire," he ground out. "I'm so close. Where can I finish?"

Cole Thomas. Even in his uncontrolled and slightly wild state, still a polite and considerate guy. Might have to see if I can break him of that, too.

Instead of answering him verbally, I took him back in my mouth, swirling my tongue around the head of his cock with my hand at the base and then resumed my rhythm, up and down the shaft. Keeping my eyes on his face, so I could see the moment he completely lost control, I took my hand away from the bottom of the shaft and pressed my finger to that place right below his balls. That was all it took, and Cole unloaded into my mouth with an especially satisfying groan.

I looked up at him as he blinked slowly down at me, trying to gather the wits I had just scattered so successfully.

"Get up here," he said hoarsely, putting a light pressure on my arms to help encourage me to slot in next to him, so he could place a light kiss on my mouth.

Chapter 18

Cole

Stunned.

That's the best word for how I felt. Ever since I had woken up just before Blaire got up to use the bathroom, with her body slotted perfectly against mine. It wasn't nearly a complex enough word to cover all the emotions coursing through me, but it covered the events that had transpired well enough. Now that my vision had fully returned and my heart rate was returning to normal, the slow kisses Blaire and I were sharing weren't going to be enough for me. I needed to know how she felt, how she smelled, how she tasted. I rolled onto my side so we were facing each other on the bed and started increasing the pressure of our kisses, luxuriating in the warmth of her mouth, the taste of Blaire mixed with my own release—a potent mixture. I moved my hands down her body and dipped my hand below the waistband of her, *no, my* shorts and into her panties.

Suddenly, Blaire was laughing against my mouth.

"What, no compliments or a thank you?" she teased, her eyes twinkling to let me know she knew exactly how much I had enjoyed her work down south.

"You're the one who prefers words and colors and charts to

communicate. Let me use my actions to communicate my appreciation," I responded lightly, all the while working my hand further into her underwear. I swiped between her legs to find her soaking wet.

"Fuck, Blaire. You loved that, didn't you?"

"There's something about seeing someone so buttoned up lose control. It just really works for me."

I circled my finger around her clit a few times before tracing the lips of her pussy. Try as she might to encourage my fingers to penetrate her opening, I evaded her goal, moving my attention to her clit. Blaire practically growled in frustration, even more so when I removed my hand, but that was only so I could pull her shorts and panties down. Blaire gamely assisted shucking them off her legs, tangling her remaining clothing in the sheets and blankets that were now a mess at the bottom of the bed.

"Come up here," I said and Blaire looked at me quizzically, until I gripped her hips and started to move her so she could sit on my face. Once she realized my intentions, she hesitated just for a moment at the intimacy of the move, but her desire won out and she moved quickly to get into position, putting a knee next to each of my ears and gripping the headboard above my head.

Then my senses were all consumed by Blaire. Her scent filled my nostrils, her thighs and glistening pussy surrounded my vision, and my hands came up to grip full handfuls of her ass as I dove in for my first taste. Licking my tongue up her entrance to her clit, I started in on my task in earnest, wanting her arousal to cover my face. I listened to her noises and breathing and learned from the way she moved when I hit certain spots what were working for her. Suddenly, her hips were moving up and down over my mouth, working with me to chase her pleasure. I heard the headboard creak from her increased grip and realized I was dying to see her expressions play out on her face. My hands left her ass, moved up her body to grip full handfuls of those glorious tits I had not given enough attention to in my haste to dive into her pussy and then

I was lifting her off me and onto her back, her head near the foot of the bed.

"Whaa—? Cole, I was so close!" Blaire whined, surprised by my sudden movement.

"I needed to see you," I said by way of explanation, spreading her legs with my shoulders and returned to my work. Acknowledging that I had edged her first ascent, I eased one finger and then a second into Blaire, groaning onto her clit when I felt that first contraction around my digits at their intrusion. My other hand snuck up to those beautiful breasts of hers, tweaking one nipple and then the other. All along I kept my eyes on Blaire's face, watching her lose the fight to keep her eyes on what I was doing down here.

Suddenly she tried to snap her legs closed and my hand that had been teasing her glorious tits came down to keep them open.

"Let go, Blaire. I've got you," I said before I could second guess it.

At this, Blaire piled both her arms over her face to keep her moans contained as she came. I felt her squeeze tightly on my fingers as I continued to work them in and out while lapping up her release. Eventually, I felt her core relax, and I removed my fingers, making eye contact. Her face freshly emerged from under her arms. I put them in my mouth and sucked, licked her clean off them. She shivered briefly.

"Now, you come here," her voice husky and soft. Our mouths met softly, creating a mixture that was uniquely us all the way through.

"Guess that sharp tongue of yours isn't only good for criticizing my spreadsheets," Blaire quipped, looking less put together and more gorgeous than I had ever seen her, eyes shining, hair mussed, and cheeks rosy.

I chuckled at this. Her sass apparently was a never ending well. We laid there, her head on my chest and my hand stroking her hair, until the heat left our bodies and the chill from the heatless room started to creep back in.

"Should we get back under the covers?" I suggested.

"Probably," Blaire answered. "I'm going to go freshen up really quick."

She clamored out of the bed, snagging one of my shirts from off the ground on her way to the bathroom. I tucked myself back into my boxers and set to work at straightening the many sheets and blankets that had become tangled during our interlude. I had tried to avoid us getting here, but it seemed inevitable. This woman had not left my mind since the first time she waltzed into my office, and the more we had gotten to know the authentic versions of each other, the stronger my attraction had become. At that moment, I decided to not ask any hard questions or over-think things too much. We were in a snow globe of a situation for tonight and I could face tomorrow tomorrow.

Snow globe of a situation? She is *getting to you, Thomas.*

The door to the bathroom opened quietly and Blaire walked slowly toward the bed, a look of uncertainty on her face that looked unfamiliar on her features.

"Come on, Blaire, it's for survival, remember?" trying to urge her with my tone to not think about it too much, either. That seemed to be the reminder Blaire needed, and she climbed back into bed and right into my arms without any hesitation, pulling my arm around her waist. I slotted us back together in that perfect-fit way I had woken to what seemed like ages ago and took a deep breath of Blaire's hair, closed my eyes, and fell asleep faster than I had in years.

Chapter 19

Blaire

I found myself blinking awake on a sunny December morning. This time, I knew where I was and exactly where the warmth I was feeling was coming from: Cole Thomas, the Winterberry Glen CFO, who I was absolutely under no circumstances supposed to have a romantic relationship with, had his body pressed against mine, while my face was buried in his chest. His arm was over my hips, keeping me locked in against him, and I felt the slow rise and fall of his chest as his sleeping body had the nerve to be hard and chiseled against mine, like a perfect fit.

Okay. I thought, *so, last night happened. We broke rule number four for the festival and also broke my record for most powerful orgasm ever. This can't ever happen again, right? The festival is too important to me, and Cole's new job is too important to him. Plus, it's another man working in government. I can't go there again. We'll just wake up and leave here and . . .*

"I can hear you thinking, Blaire."

A deep and sleepy voice spoke from above my head. Guess those slow, deep breaths weren't exactly sleeping breaths after all. Cole disentangled himself from me slightly, leaning back to brush my hair away from my face and look into my eyes.

"Want to share any of those thoughts out loud?"

I definitely didn't want to share *all* of them out loud, so I went with the second to last one. I'd never had this sort of direct talk with a partner before, but Cole wasn't my normal type of sexual encounter, so I summoned my big girl bravery and looked up into his eyes.

"I'm a rule follower, and while last night was a great time, I don't want you to suffer the consequences of a personal relationship with me and cost yourself this job. So, I think we just need to let last night melt away with the snow that's hopefully clear from the highway by now."

I realized I had said all of that really fast, without taking a breath, and Cole was looking at me with amusement. Among that amusement, his eyes seemed to display a flicker of disappointment for just a brief moment. But then he was back to the serious Cole Thomas I was used to, just paired with a warm smile that was new to me.

"You're probably right, and not only is there my job to think about, but how important it is for you to stand on your own and succeed with this festival. I wouldn't want anyone to get the wrong idea about how the festival planning process may have been impacted by our relationship. I'll head downstairs and see if I can get an update from Louise on the status of the highways."

Cole hesitated for a moment and then leaned forward to press a soft kiss on the top of my head. Even though we both had acknowledged this thing between us couldn't continue outside of this bed, I closed my eyes for a brief second and breathed him in, appreciating he had taken a moment to close out our encounter, before switching gears to our professional relationship.

Cole slid out of bed and bent to pick up his T-shirt and sweatpants, facing the window and away from the bed. I allowed myself to admire that ass in those briefs one last time—I'm professional, but still a human—before wrenching my eyes away and picking up my phone for the first time since last night. As I was scrolling through my notifications, Cole silently slipped from the room, leaving me truly alone for the first time in twenty-four hours.

Among the myriad of weather notifications and texts from my parents acknowledging my messages letting them know we had gotten off the road and were safe, were texts from Charlotte.

Charlotte (10:45 p.m.): Did you guys make it home okay? It's wild out there! I'm not sure our deliveries are going to make it to the store in the morning.

Charlotte (11:07 p.m.): Oh my god, wait. I started a new romance novel before bed (my toxic trait, you know) and there was a mix-up at the destination wedding resort and the maid of honor and best man who hate each other are booked into the same room. My BFF senses are tingling. ARE YOU AND COLE STRANDED IN THE SNOW AND SHARING A ROOM. ARE HIS FOREARMS THERE TOO?

Charlotte (12:07 a.m.): Okay, going to bed now, slightly worried, mostly hopeful. Text me ASAP!

I shook my head at Charlotte's antics and opened the text chain to respond back.

Blaire (7:58 a.m.): We're okay! We did not make it home. We ended up at the most Christmassy B&B you've ever seen. *2 photos attached.*

Charlotte (7:59 a.m.): I feel like you're burying the lede here, B. WAS THERE ONLY ONE BED?!

Blaire (8:01 a.m.): I may or may not be sitting in that one bed. Wearing Cole's shirt. And only his shirt...

Charlotte (8:02 a.m.): *Fainting girl.gif*

Blaire (8:03 a.m.): But we're never speaking of it again. It was a snowstorm-only happening. We both have goals we need to focus on.

Charlotte (8:05 a.m.): *cough * Bullshit! *cough*. That sounds very responsible of you both. Dig your way over to the bookstore later so you can point out the book that best mimics the scene you're never speaking of again?

Blaire (8:07 a.m.): I hate you. Gotta go, hear him coming back to the room. See you soon.

Charlotte (8:08 a.m.): *Winking emoji* *Heart emoji* *Eggplant Emoji*

Shaking my head at my best friend and her antics, I pulled up a local news website just as Cole opened the door. Plausible deniability, ya know? I looked up at him, only to see he had a slightly pained looked on his face as he walked into the room. I opened my mouth to ask what was wrong, when I noticed he wasn't alone. Louise was behind him carrying a tray of breakfast sandwiches and hot coffee.

"Thank goodness the power came back on a few hours ago, so we could brew coffee and cook up some sandwiches! Your mister here tried to say you all didn't need anything special, but after the mix-up with the room last night, I just thought I could bring the breakfast part of the B&B to you! You sure look cozy there in that bed! Everyone sleep okay?!"

I clutched the blankets secure above my waist, suddenly incredibly aware of the fact that I had Cole's shirt on and *nothing* else. I shared a look with Cole, who had an expression on his face that I recognized: murderous intent. Uncomfortable as Louise's observation and over-enthusiastic breakfast delivery was, I found myself biting back a laugh. The whole situation was just slightly ridiculous and out of control. Guess I was in a good mood. Blame it on the post-orgasm endorphins.

"Thanks so much, Louise. That's so thoughtful," I managed to get out with a straight face. "If you want, set the tray on the foot of the bed here. We're going to be hitting the road soon, so these to-go cups are just perfect."

Louise, a smile beaming on her face, walked into the room and set the tray on the bed. I noticed her clock my underwear on the floor—okay, now the endorphins weren't quite enough to keep my good humor anymore—and walked out of the door saying, "Thank you so much for staying with us. *Come* back anytime!"

This time I couldn't withhold my laughter. As soon as the door shut behind her, the dirty bird, my laugh burst out of me and I was surprised to hear Cole's chuckle joining mine. He had such a nice laugh, warm and chesty.

I bolted out of bed, pulling the oversized shirt I was wearing down to my mid-thigh, needing to get dressed, get out of this room, and get my mind reset to the professional relationship with Cole. I bent down to pick up the offending underwear and grab my dress, tights, and bra that I had left laying on a chair last night.

"I'll, uh, just go change in the bathroom."

I looked back at Cole as I said this and noticed his eyes were on my legs, before jerking them up to meet mine.

"Sounds good. Louise let me know that the plows were working double time overnight and we should be all set to make the rest of the trip home. So maybe we'll just take these sandwiches and coffee to go and get home? I want to go check on my mom ASAP."

Seems like I wasn't the only one who needed to leave this room and the memories we had created in it. I turned and went into the bathroom, smiling at myself in the mirror, realizing Cole had shared something private about himself this morning, without any wine and even in the light of day. I knew that going back to our professional relationship was the right call for both of us, but was glad to know we wouldn't be leaving behind everything we found at The Old Coach Inn.

Chapter 20

December 8

   Cole

It had been a week since the blizzard and it appeared Blaire and I were successful in our goal of transitioning back to our professional, if not friendlier, relationship with each other.

Well, I should be honest. Blaire seemed to do a good job of relating to me in public and I felt like I was putting up a pretty convincing front. I would also absolutely be lying if I didn't admit to a few shower sessions where I conjured up the way it felt to have Blaire sit on my face, recalling just how sweet she had tasted. But that was in the shower, and showers ran on water, and snow was a form of water, so it was basically a snowstorm loophole. Never quite as satisfied as I had been in that king-sized bed, as soon as I stepped out of that shower, it was back to being Cole Thomas, CFO, whose job it was to oversee the financial status of the Holly Ridge Christmas Festival and stay emotionally distant from any brunette festival planners I may encounter.

The thing was though, the festival was honestly mostly planned. We knew what the expenses were going to be at this point. Of course, there would be some last-minute things Blaire would need my approval for, but that could happen over the phone or by email. So why was I here in Holly Ridge, freezing my ass off, watching a tree get decorated in the town square?

"Cole! You're here!"

I felt my heart skip a beat to hear Blaire calling my name, even just in greeting—so much for emotionally distant—and I turned around to see her walking toward the town square from Jitters, two coffee cups in hand.

"The assistant CFO is handling all the year-end work, since I've been so tied up with the festival, so I found myself in the office with nothing to do and thought I would pop over and see how things were going."

What I didn't say out loud was how I was essentially setting up our assistant CFO to take over my job in just a few weeks, but I could tell by the knowing look in Blaire's eyes, she hadn't missed that unspoken truth. She looked like she wanted to ask me more, but our newly re-established professional parameters were stopping her.

"Well, we're happy to have you over here. I'm sure we'll find something for you to do. Peppermint Chocolate Mocha? Susie makes her own syrup, so they're delicious and just like Christmas in a cup."

Blaire held out her left hand to me, offering me a cup of coffee.

"You didn't buy that second one for someone else?"

"Susie doesn't let me pay for my own coffee at this point, so I always grab a second one of whatever I'm getting so she'll run my card and I can tip high. I figure in this cold, someone will be willing to take something warm."

If anyone ever asked, I would say I took it because it was so fucking cold outside, but internally, I just wanted a piece of anything that was important to Blaire, even if it was just her favorite coffee.

"Sure, I'll try it. I'm not one for sugary drinks, but you are right, it is damn cold out here."

I took the coffee, our gloved fingers brushing. I probably

imagined the heat that traveled through the two layers of cloth, but when the mocha was in my hand, it didn't seem to give off as much heat as it did for that brief second when Blaire and I were both holding it together.

Blaire was looking at me expectantly, so I raised my eyebrows at her, causing her to smile, and then raised the disposable cup to my lips for a sip. Flavor and warmth exploded on my tongue, and I could sort of see what Blaire meant by 'Christmas in a cup.' Lowering the drink, I licked some of the foam from my lips, noticing that Blaire's eyes were following my tongue's path. Maybe that professional I wasn't quite so easy for Blaire after all.

"I don't know that I would order it regularly for myself, but you're right. That is pretty good."

Blaire's eyes left my mouth and moved up to meet my gaze, seeming warmed by my approval of her favorite Christmas drink. She was about to respond when we were interrupted by an older gentleman.

"Ms. Greene, there's an issue with the lamppost decorations that we need you to take a look at. And also, the guys with the ice rink are here to start setting up."

Blaire switched on her festival planner mode instantly, nodding at the man.

"Thanks so much, Todd. I'll go meet the Ice, Ice Baby Rinks crew and be sure they have everything they need to get started, and then head over to the lamppost crew and check in with them."

"Why don't I go meet with the ice rink guys, it sounds like that lamppost decoration problem could be pretty urgent, depending on what's going on." Suddenly helping with the ice rink and keeping Blaire away from anyone who may have come with the rinks to install them seemed like a perfect use of my time.

Blaire smirked at me knowingly, probably remembering the same thing I was—how our initial meeting with Rick had gone over the summer—but surprisingly she didn't fight me on it. Even if we were pretending it hadn't happened, I definitely couldn't stand the idea of watching Rick and his whole Blaire Bear routine after knowing how perfectly *Blaire Bear* and I fit together.

"Thanks, Cole, that'll be a big help. I'll pop over once the lamppost situation is sorted."

With that, she and Todd walked away toward a small crowd of people gathered around some big plastic tubs next to a light pole in front of the town post office. I watched her grab her clipboard out of her bag and go over a few other things with Todd on the way, and I had to once again admire her organization and that she was just damn good at her job.

All at once I realized I was standing still, in the middle of a Christmas festival, holding a Christmassy-themed drink and headed to talk to a man about a temporary ice rink.

Only for Blaire Greene, I thought to myself, heading over to the parking lot where the Ice, Ice Baby Rinks trucks were parked.

Blaire

It was one thing after another that needed my attention that morning.

After the lamppost decorations were sorted out—the fuse in the light strings just needed to be replaced—the Christmas Market vendor stalls needed to be signed for, Susie needed a taste test on the final recipe for the cookie-decorating contest—anytime Susie, anytime—and a million other small details flowed my way. This was honestly what I lived for, the final days before a festival opened, when months of planning and hard work seemed to come together.

What was different this time was the awareness I had of where Cole was the entire morning. I wasn't even entirely sure why he was here, but what I was sure about was the way I felt my heart flutter in my chest when I saw him standing there in my town square, gazing at that Christmas tree. Oh sure, I knew what sort of professional affect I was projecting, but it was only my love for this town and this festival that was keeping me from melting into a pile of goo over memories of *that night* on a regular basis. I prided myself on being a woman who put herself and her career first, which is why I had put forward the suggestion that we leave those wonderful, mind-blowing, orgasmic activities behind in that room. But Cole was testing all my pre-existing rules and patterns. And when I looked him in the eye as I handed him my extra peppermint mocha? It certainly made me wonder if he was just projecting his professional outward appearance toward me as well.

I couldn't help comparing Cole to Mason, the government official I had dated in one of my previous towns. He would never be caught dead outside in temperate weather working on festival setup, let alone on a cold day like today. Now that my rose-colored glasses were removed, Mason was only interested in being around the festival when he could interject in front of someone important, whether it be the mayor or the press, to take credit for my work and my accomplishments. Even though the next job I took was only in the next county, my usefulness to Mason ended when my contract did and he unceremoniously dumped me for one of the reporters who had always been making eyes at him during our press conferences.

I'm not sure I would admit it to Cole's face anytime soon, but it was honestly a huge help to have him around. He knew the schedule and the details almost as well as I did, so since I couldn't be in more than one place at a time, it was comforting to know he was in some of those places for me instead. And I was surprised to find that I trusted him to stand in for me; while Cole might not get Christmas, he does get organization and details, so I knew he wouldn't let anything slip through.

After he was done overseeing the ice rink unloading—Rick wasn't scheduled to be here today, but I didn't let Cole know that ahead of time. I may trust him with my festival schedule, but that doesn't mean I can't have a little fun, right?—Cole migrated back to where the vendor stalls were being unloaded and was helping the Merry Market crew space out the stalls according to the diagram I had worked up. Occasionally, when I found my gaze wandering toward him, I found him looking back at me as well. Seems like I wasn't the only one who was aware of my surroundings today.

We danced around each other in the town square all morning, until I had to go into the community center to meet with the volunteers that would be manning the festival headquarters over the next few weeks. We went over frequently asked questions, first aid and emergency procedures, and then ran through the brochure I had produced to hand out to visitors and guests. I was fielding questions from the volunteers when I noticed Cole standing in the back of the room, paper bag in hand. I caught his eye and raised my eyebrow in question to him, which he answered with a small wave, leaning his back against the wall, and pulling out his phone, indicating he was planning to wait there until I was done. Wrapping up with the volunteers, I left them with the sign-up sheets for coverage shifts and made my way back toward Cole.

"I noticed you hadn't stopped for anything to eat and it's well past lunchtime, so I went into Jitters, found Susie behind the counter, and asked her what your favorite sandwich was and had her make you one. Actually, I had her make two and I can see why you love the chicken salad croissant so much. It was delicious."

"That's two instances of Holly Ridge food and drink in one day, Thomas. You going to be okay?" I teased as I grabbed the paper bag from him.

"But thanks for doing that. You're right, I've just been going, going all day. I hadn't realized how hungry I had gotten and may not have stopped to grab something if I was left to my own devices."

His mouth curled into a soft smile, the corner of his eyes crinkling to cap off the pleased look on his face.

"You're welcome, Greene. I guess I'm open to trying out new things recently."

The innuendo sat between us like a roaring fire, trying to melt the ice wall we had built between us with all the reasons and circumstances we couldn't act on this attraction that was becoming impossible to ignore anytime we were together. As much as I wanted to stoke it, the room full of Holly Ridge residents around us and the official roles we played for the festival were too present in the room to allow me to do so.

"Well, my stomach appreciates it. Passing out would not be a good look for a festival planner."

The light in Cole's eyes dimmed slightly when I didn't grab at the chestnut roasting stick he had metaphorically offered me, with an expression of resigned understanding passing over his face. Then it was back to tight-ass-Cole demeanor, very official and distant.

"I've got to head back to Winterberry Glen to get ready for dinner with my mom. I'm telling her about the job tonight, so figured I would actually cook something tonight instead of picking up food. That shouldn't tip her off or anything."

Apparently, the Cole in front of me was not as distant as appearances would have me believe. I was glad that even though I had shut down the flirtation avenue moments ago, Cole was still sharing with me.

"Good luck with that conversation, and with the cooking. I guess I'll see you around?"

He nodded and started walking backward out of the community center, hands in his pockets and eyes on mine.

"I'll probably be back to check on setup again sometime this week. Let me know if anything comes up you need me for."

I lifted the hand not holding the paper bag in a wave before he finally turned around and pushed out the front door, realizing for the first time the truth in the statement "I hated to watch him go, but loved to watch him leave."

Chapter 21

Cole

I stood at the stove in my mom's kitchen, mindlessly stirring the sauce that was simmering along, while the noodles cooked in a boiling pot on the next burner. Yes, cooking for me often meant pasta, but the sauce was made from scratch with my mom's family recipe, so it was technically homemade. I hadn't had much call for learning how to cook as an adult, eating dinner on my own most nights, so I took pride in my sauce making. Mom told me it was even better than hers, but I think that might have been her mom-goggles talking.

While at the stove, I let my mind wander back to the last interaction Blaire and I had earlier today. I thought about how I had seen the warring in her eyes after my impulsive acknowledgment to the new things we had tried together over the past week. If you would have asked me nine months ago who would be having a harder time keeping their attraction tamped down, well, first I would have laughed at the idea that Blaire and I could actually share a space without fighting, but I would have definitely bet on Blaire being the one to struggle, not me. I had worked fastidiously to keep my emotions locked down since the day my dad walked out, and the fact that I let the reins loosen even slightly around Blaire should have been even more of a reason to stay away.

But what I had learned about Blaire was that her discipline in keeping our relationship professional wasn't coming completely from a place of insane-level self-control, but more from a place where she cared so much about others. It wasn't lost on me that the reasoning that came out of her mouth when she word-vomited about why we couldn't repeat the actions of the night of the snowstorm wasn't focused on her own reputation or self-preservation. No, it was for me and the job I had lined up. The job that would take me away from her, from our towns, and the life that I had always known.

Speaking of the life I had always known, I shook myself and focused on the near-boiling-over pot of pasta on the stove and tried to bring myself back to the here and now—this here and now being when I had to tell my mom I was leaving her and moving away for a job.

"I can hear the pasta bubbling in there, son, and the sauce smells just about perfect. Should I set the table and grab us some drinks?"

Mom stood in the doorway between the kitchen and the living room, placemats in hand, ready to set the table no matter what I said, apparently.

"Sure, Mom, that would be great. I brought a bottle of red over to have with dinner. It's open and breathing over there on the counter."

Mom walked over to the small table in the corner of the kitchen that we used for meals, laying out her favorite gingham placemats and matching napkins and then walked over to the cupboard to grab our bowls and set them on the counter next to where I was cooking at the stove. She wandered a few steps to her left, picked up the bottle of wine and examined the label.

"This looks like a pretty good bottle for Winterberry Glen. I'm sure when you move to the city, you'll have access to even better wine than you can get around here."

Glad I hadn't been holding either pot of bubbling hot liquids at that moment in time, I stared at my mom, dumbfounded.

"Well, I figured that's what you were planning to tell me about tonight after you put in all this effort making your sauce for me. You seemed nervous. You were stirring that pot of pasta an awful lot. I thought I might put you out of your misery."

"Wait, you knew about the move? How?!"

My mom looked back at me, a look that said, "I love my son, but he can be a real idiot."

"You and Austin seem to think just because you're in a different room there's a soundproof force field or something up. My hearing isn't *that* bad, you know. And that boy's voice just has a way of carrying."

With that, she poured us each a healthy portion of wine into glasses she seemed to have procured out of thin air and walked herself to the table to sit down.

I went through the motions of straining the pasta and serving our preferred portions into our favorite large bowls, spooning sauce onto the top of each pile of pasta. I brought the bowls over to the table and sat down.

"I want to know all about the move and this new job I'm assuming you're moving for, but first, don't forget the garlic bread."

Apparently, Mom had it all together tonight, and I couldn't be trusted with anything. I jumped up, grabbing the garlic bread out of the oven—somehow remembering to grab an oven mitt first. I threw the toasted bread into the basket she kept on top of the fridge for such occasions.

"Why didn't you tell me you knew?"

Mom arched her eyebrow at me. I always forget that's where I had picked up that move.

"Why didn't you tell me about the move earlier?"

Point to the matriarch.

"It wasn't 100 percent a sure thing until my trip up to the capital last week. The whole festival was basically a trial run for the position they have in mind for me, and they're pleased with how things have gone so far, so we had a meeting to sort out some of the final perks and package details when we were there. I didn't think it was worth mentioning until I knew it was a sure thing. I didn't want to upset you unnecessarily."

Mom continued to eat her pasta while she thought this over, and I realized I've hardly touched mine. While I took a bite, she responded, "We'll come back to that in a minute. Now, tell me why you want to take this job. The whole story, please."

I guess eating my pasta was going to have to wait until the questioning was over. Why didn't I know how to make a simpler-to-eat-while-interrogated food?!

"Well, there are a few reasons, I guess. The first is that it's a promotion. You can't go much higher than CFO in a town this size, and it would be nice to not have peaked in my career at thirty. And, also, honestly, a big part of it is the memories of this town. There's the bad blood between Winterberry Glen and Holly Ridge, the feelings associated with being here after Dad left and . . ."

"And how it felt to live here while he was still here, too?"

"I mean, yeah, a little. From the outside, everyone thinks these small towns are the perfect place to live, and everyone that lives here is happy to do so. I've never really had a reason to feel that way. I love living close to you and Austin, but that's really all I have here. I guess I want a chance to find more?"

At this, I found myself needing a big swig from that wineglass. Another mistake because that's when Mom dropped the big Greene bomb.

"And what about that festival planner? You don't have her to keep you here?"

I spluttered on my swig of wine. Damn Austin and his big mouth.

"Have her? I've never had her. I mean, I don't have her in any capacity except our official working capacity. She's a competent coworker, though a little too into Christmas for my tastes, you know how I feel about Christmas, but nope, she's definitely not a reason for me to stay in Winterberry Glen or Holly Ridge or anywhere near here."

Smooth, Cole. Really smooth.

I can tell Mom is trying not to laugh at me.

"Okay, fine, so Blaire isn't a reason for you to stay. So, let's go back to you not wanting to tell me about the possibility of you moving because you didn't want to upset me. Do you really think I'm that unable to take care of myself? That you're the only support network I have?"

"Well, no Mom, of course not, but . . ."

"No buts. You're right, Cole. We don't talk about it much, but for several years after your dad left, I wasn't the most self-sufficient parent around. And I'm sorry I put you through that. But when you stayed here for college instead of taking those offers from more prestigious universities that would allow you to start your life somewhere else, I decided I was going to make a change. And then when you took the job here in Winterberry Glen? Well, that's what moved me to start therapy. I wanted that to be the last time you made a decision with my well-being ahead of your own. So, Cole, if the move to the capital and taking this new job with the state government is going to make you happy, of course I'll miss our weekly dinners, but you're not the only man in my life, you know. And family isn't just the group of people you're born into. Now, go heat up that pasta. I made tiramisu for dessert."

I got up to put the bowl in the microwave on autopilot. It had been a long time since my mom had delivered such an impassioned speech directed at me, and it was going to take some time to process it all. There was one part I needed clarification on.

"I am sure Austin would love to continue weekly dinners with you too, Mom, and would definitely be willing to help with whatever you need."

"That's not the type of man in my life I was talking about, Cole, and you know it. Stop trying to be cute. It was time for me to take an emotional risk again and I think maybe you could consider doing the same. Think about letting someone in."

Mom was just delivering thought grenades left and right today.

"Oh, and he's a big Christmas type. I think I want to get a Christmas tree this year. You and I can go pick one out sometime this week, if you have time with the festival and packing and move prepping, that is. We'll need a new tree stand and probably could spring for some new lights and ornaments too. I'm sure it's been—"

"Twenty years since you've had a tree. Sure thing, Mom. We can definitely make time for all of that. Opening night of the festival is still a few days away. Let's plan to go tomorrow."

"Sounds great Cole, I'm looking forward to it. I think it's time we gave a lot of things another chance in this household, Christmas being one of them."

Mom sat back in her chair, swirling her glass of wine, looking very satisfied with the way the evening's conversation had gone. That made one of us, at least. I couldn't remember the last time a conversation plan went so far off the rails.

A tree? A new man? Second chances? Asking me about a girl? Man. Times, they sure are a-changing.

Chapter 22

December 15

Blaire

It was finally here: opening night of the festival. Somehow the last nine months had dragged on and yet also flown by in the time it took a snowflake to melt once it landed on warm skin.

I didn't have to worry about my Christmas movie-themed nightmares anymore, because I was barely sleeping at this point. Susie was going to have to put a daily maximum on the amount of peppermint mochas I was allowed to consume, because the sugar, anxiety, and caffeine coursing through my body were not sustainable for the next two weeks.

Opening night of the festival always began with the tree lighting ceremony. Everyone would gather in the square around the gazebo and the huge Norway Spruce tree. The hot chocolate, mulled wine, and toasted nut vendors in the Christmas Market were open for people to buy something warm to hold on to while they waited for the ceremony to start. The rest of the vendors were prepping behind their stall shutters, with the market officially opening as soon as the tree was lit. Holiday music was being piped from the newly installed speaker system in the gazebo, thanks to a generous donation from Mike's Speaker Shack, and the air buzzed with Christmas spirit and eager anticipation of getting the festival underway.

In years past, the ceremony had probably been too long and full of unnecessary pomp and circumstance. This year's would feature a welcome address from yours truly, a medley from the local high school marching band while people got into position, a countdown to build the anticipation and then lights would be on, and the festival would be off and running. Tradition said that the mayor acted as the one to push the button controlling the thousands of lights strung around Norm—Norm the Norway Spruce, yes—and Rudolph had done so as chair of the city council in years past. This year, in a little show of spite to the council, as well as a push for publicity, I held a contest, inviting youth from all over the tristate area to pen a holiday poem. The planning committee had voted for their favorite poem, and the winner would have the chance to read their poem right before the countdown, and then push the button to turn on the tree. Pretty genius, right?

We had, of course, received lots of entries from the youth of Holly Ridge, as well as those from outside of the county and even the state. Sadly, there were no entries from any Winterberry Glen youth. Knowing what I knew now about the origins of the feud I probably shouldn't have been as surprised as I was. I had removed the names and home locations from poems before the judging, so no one knew that fact except me, but I had made a mental note to reach out directly to the Winterberry Glen elementary school if—no—when there was another festival next year.

The winner ended up being little Olive Martinez, aged eight, from a few counties over. She wrote a poem from the point of view of Norm—someone, or someone's parents had done their research—that the committee just ate up and we had it printed on some souvenir coffee mugs and tote bags that were available for sale at the festival. Olive was present and accounted for, along with her parents, and was practicing her poem in a corner of the gazebo with the encouragement of her dad and stepmom.

It was inching closer and closer to 6:00 p.m., the time when the tree lighting ceremony would kick off, and I was going over my opening night checklist one more time when I heard Cole's deep voice behind me.

"It looks like there's a pretty good-sized crowd gathered out there."

He was right. There weren't official attendance records from the past few years—because of course there weren't—but it looked like the crowd was bigger than the estimates I had badgered all the square businesses for this summer when I was setting my attendance goals for each major event.

"Yes, I'm really pleased with the size of things. Moving the tree lighting to Friday night was definitely the right call, allowing us to kick off the festival strong on the eve of the weekend."

I was still looking at my checklist, definitely not because I was avoiding looking at Cole's face because I knew what it would do to my concentration, but really because I wanted to check everything over a third time. Only twice? What does Santa know?

"Uh, I brought you something."

This made me turn around and look at the hand he was holding out toward me. Nestled in the black leather glove he was wearing was a to-go coffee cup from Berry Good Coffee. Before raising my eyes to meet his, I took in the rest of his outfit. His usual go-to slacks were present, and he was wearing a puffy coat open over an emerald half-zip sweater. I couldn't tell what level on the just-fucked scale his hair was today, as he had an adorable grey beanie pulled down over his ears, really completing the whole business-guy-goes-to-Aspen vibe he had going on.

"I know you're partial to Jitters' peppermint mochas, but I thought I'd pay you back for the coffee from last week. And I figured you might need a break from the sugar rush. This is my favorite winter drink. A flat white with cinnamon sprinkled on top."

"Oh. Thanks. I mean, you did get me lunch last week. But I

showed you mine . . . I mean, my favorite drink, so I'm happy to try yours."

Cole looked guarded as I brought the cup to my mouth, taking a cautious sip in case it was still scalding hot. After all the things we had shared with each other, it seemed that opening up to taste something that was his "favorite" was still an uncomfortable situation for him. The coffee was smooth and a little bitter, with the cinnamon adding a warm, distinct flavor to the overall profile. Forget Christmas in a cup. This drink was Cole in a cup.

"Wow, Cole, this is good. I may see if I can shock Susie by ordering it sometime instead of my usual."

Cole smiled a relieved smile, pleased that he had shared another part of himself with me and I hadn't thrown it back in his face.

"So, how are things going? All ready for the tree lighting?"

"Yes, I think I am. I never get over the nerves of speaking in front of a large group of people, but once I get up there and get going, I'll be fine."

"You know this festival and this town inside and out, and you get to talk about Christmas in an appropriate setting in front of people who are definitely interested. I think you were made for this opportunity."

Even though he had gotten in a little dig about my Christmas enthusiasm, I could tell by looking in Cole's eyes that the encouragement was sincere, and I felt my shoulders loosen a bit more, knowing he was here and on my side.

"So, did you come just to deliver coffee and a little bit of snark mixed with encouragement? Or are you actually here to stay for the tree lighting ceremony?"

Cole chuckled at me calling him out, but his eyes twinkled when he knew his pep talk had been well received.

"I thought I might stay for the ceremony, and also see if you need anything else. I can imagine that opening night must be another time you wish you could be in five places at once."

How right he was.

"Well, if you're offering, it would honestly be great to have you post up in the community command center for tonight. I think my volunteers have got things covered, but it being the first night, it would be nice to have a little back-up there. Then you'd be out of the cold too. Doesn't the night air seep right through those slacks? Ever heard of jeans?"

That amused look still on his face, Cole continued to laugh at me. Honestly, he should really know that only encourages me by now.

"I'm happy to sit in the community center so you can be out here amid all your people. I may even have to take off a layer or two. I've got long johns on underneath here."

The satisfied smirk on his face as we maintained eye contact let me know he was completely aware that my brain was battling between an image of him shirking off some layers or that ass in tight long john fabric. The moment was broken by Leroy, the tech guy I had hired to make sure everything ran smoothly tonight.

"Ms. Greene, I'm sorry to interrupt, but it's 5:57 and you said you wanted to start at 6:00 sharp. Should I cut the music here in about two minutes?"

I took another sip of the Cole-in-a-cup drink that was rapidly cooling in my hand to gather myself before turning to face Leroy, all Christmas festival business focused once again.

"Thanks, Leroy, that'll be perfect. And again, please, call me Blaire."

Cole was still standing to my left and sensing that I was back in the festival zone, stuffed his hands in his pocket.

"Well, I'll head out to the edge of the crowd so I can hear your welcome speech, and then book it over to the community center so I'm there when the lights are on and things get underway."

I was glad that Cole would hear my festival intro but couldn't help but be disappointed he wasn't going to stay to watch the poem and the light countdown. But no matter how many times I tried to trick him into a festive spirit, Christmas just wasn't his thing, and I wasn't going to force it.

"That'll be great. There's a walkie-talkie in the center you can reach me on if you need me during the evening."

At this, Cole turned and walked down the gazebo steps, and I rearranged the papers on my clipboard, so my opening remarks were front and center, even though I had been writing them since the day the council called about the job last winter.

Right at 5:59, the music cut out, and I made my way down the gazebo steps to the small stage we had erected next to the Christmas tree. A hush fell over the crowd briefly when they noticed the music was no longer playing over the speakers, then a buzz of excitement and anticipation arose as the townspeople and visitors alike anticipated getting the festival underway. I noticed my parents, sister, brother-in-law, Brad, and the twins were in the front of the crowd. I made eye contact with my dad while he beamed at me, knowing this was a culmination of a lot of work and planning.

At 6:00 p.m. on the dot, I approached the microphone, took a deep breath, tucked my hair behind my ear with my free hand, and got ready to set the train off down the tracks.

"Hello everyone, and welcome to the 116th annual Holly Ridge Christmas Festival! My name is Blaire Greene and I have the distinct honor of being your Holly Ridge Christmas Festival planner this year! I was born and raised right here in Holly Ridge and grew up coming to these festivals with my parents and friends. I wanted to honor the traditions of the festival that many of us know and love, while moving it forward to welcome and draw in a new generation of festival lovers like Olive Martinez, who you'll hear from in just a minute. All the businesses around the square are done up in their holiday best to welcome you in, the Christmas Market right here will open as soon as the tree lights are on, and the ice rink is smooth and polished, just waiting for you to glide on it, over next to Al's General Store. We have gingerbread houses and a history of the festival waiting for you to view in the community center, along with first aid and festival service volunteers should you need anything while you're here. A special event of some sort is planned each day and night, leading up to the Gingerbread Ball on New Year's Eve—tickets are still available!"

I took a deep breath, wishing I could see Cole's face before I delivered the next, more emotional, part of my welcome. This part I had been mulling over since our research adventure to the Winterberry Glen library and had finally found the words just in the last two weeks.

"As I said, this festival was a huge part of my life growing up. It was a time when it felt like the whole world came together to celebrate the magic of Christmas. There was special music, special food, special friends, special bedtimes—it was just a sparkling and shimmering month I looked forward to every single year. As some of you may know, it's possible this may be the very last Holly Ridge Christmas Festival. I'm hoping that is not the case because I want future generations of Holly Ridge residents and those from surrounding towns and communities to experience what I did growing up. I've learned recently that my red-and-green-colored glasses viewing the festival as a welcoming and magical place may not always have been completely accurate, so I hope that those of you who are here tonight and across the span of the festival will remember that Christmas is a time to open our hearts to everyone, no matter where they're from, and welcome them to our town to enjoy our festival."

"And now, please enjoy a Christmas medley from our very own Holly Ridge Marching Pines!"

Did I intentionally plan a not-so-veiled message about inclusivity at our festival right before a marching band started playing, which would be followed by a child reading a poem? Of course, I did. No one is going to heckle children—at least I hoped not—and hopefully the twinkling of the lights immediately following the poem would soften any prickly edges I had raised.

After the band played and Olive read her poem, with more confidence than I had ever had at age eight, the countdown began.

"10, 9, 8, 7, 6, 5, 4, 3, 2, 1!"

Olive smashed the button with a bit more vigor than necessary, but she was excited—who could blame her—and the lights on the town's Norway Spruce came to life. This was the signal for businesses and the lamppost's decorations to turn on, and all around us was a host of bright lights and decorations, brightening the square with Christmas cheer.

"Enjoy the festival, everyone. Merry Christmas!" I said into the microphone as I waved to the already dispersing crowd, eager to get in line at the skating rink, refill their mulled wine mugs, or duck into the community center to get warm and check out those gingerbread houses. H&H were leading Gretchen and Brad off to the front of the skating rink line so fast I'm surprised their feet weren't blurring like the Road Runner's. For the first time since my speech ended, I looked back at Dad to see what he thought of my slightly off-brand messaging. He nodded at me, his face even more full of pride than it had been when I took the stage, and I let out a breath I wasn't aware I was holding. Of course, I wanted the town to be proud of me, but at the end of the day, the approval of that man meant a whole lot more.

Chapter 23

Cole

The festival was off and running.

Blaire's message about welcoming everyone into the festival was running through my head. Did she add that line because of my experience at the festival so many years ago? Did Blaire actually believe the festival was the path to take to end a decades-old rivalry that had started with a festival?

There wasn't much time to ponder these existential queries, because suddenly, the community center was full of activity and people asking questions. Blaire was right, her volunteers knew their stuff and handled everything competently, but it was nice to be the extra body to direct people coming into the center to the right places, show them where they could drop off their gingerbread house competition voting sheets, and step-in to provide bathroom and dinner breaks for the volunteers.

The market and ice rink were scheduled to close at 11:00 p.m. on weekend nights, so things finally quieted down after 10:00 p.m. Volunteers packed up and headed home, Blaire correctly anticipated the shift needs for her rotations so as not to burn people out, and after a while, I found myself wandering over to the section of the community center that displayed the history of the festival. I thought back to that fateful festival twenty years ago —remembering all the twinkling lights, the booths decorated with garland, the town square's gazebo lit up like a Christmas beacon, the huge tree decorated and bright. I remember noticing a brown-haired girl in a bright red jacket and shiny black boots, her mittened hand gripped by an older woman who seemed to be her mother. The Christmas lights reflected brightly in her eyes as they waited in the hot chocolate line with an older man who seemed to know everyone. I remember envying that little girl. Her Christmas spirit and seemingly happy, normal family, who could all go out in public together without anyone arguing or weaving drunkenly.

I shook my head to break out of my reverie and focused back on the displays in front of me. My eyes moved over all the photos and timelines that showed when different elements of the festival had been added, taking in that Norm was actually Norm the fourth. I knew from Blaire's research that the first Norm had been stolen but had no idea a strike of lightning had taken out Norm Junior and a nasty beetle infestation had taken out Norm the third. I slowed down slightly at the photos of festivals from twenty-five years ago, which would have been the time that I was still begging my parents to come across the bridge and bring me to experience the jolliness of the festival first-hand.

Part of me was tempted to exit the exhibit before we hit the festival that ended all Christmas spirit for me, but a picture of a bright red coat caught my eye. I stepped closer and saw her, the girl with the brown hair, red coat, and shiny black boots from twenty years ago. She wasn't holding the woman's hand in the photo, but the older woman and the older man from my memory were in the background of the photo, which focused on the little girl with her hot chocolate, clutched tightly between her mittened hands and joy on her face after taking what I editorialized to be the very first sip. Pulling my eyes away from the girl in the photo, I took in the faces of the adults in the photo, startling to realize that I was looking at a younger, but unmistakably accurate, photo of former Mayor Greene. Did that mean?

My eyes swung to the left of the photo where the image explanation was written.

"Festival Planner Blaire Greene with her parents, former Mayor William 'Bill' Greene and Evelyn Greene, after the Christmas Tree Lighting Ceremony."

I couldn't believe it. The little girl, who I had admittedly thought of less and less over the years, but I could still picture with alarming clarity whenever I put myself to the task, was none other than Blaire. The woman who had brought Christmas back into my life, even through a work obligation, after I had worked so hard to keep it out for so long was the one who had inspired so much of my holiday envy over the years.

Suddenly, I needed to see her. Realizing I was somehow the only one left in the room, I put my coat, hat, and gloves back on, turned off all the lights, and strode out of the community center with urgency. I vaguely remembered Blaire saying something about the doors being on timers that could be set remotely, so I hoped they locked behind me, but I didn't have time to turn around and check. I had to find her.

I stopped on the edge of the square that had apparently turned into a ghost town in the time between me getting lost in the past, the festival ending, and now. Except there was one extremely familiar feminine figure standing in front of the Christmas tree, illuminated in the bright, white glowing lights. I couldn't even be mad about the cost of electricity to run that many lights. Blaire had sourced a solar generator that had been storing energy for weeks now. Even if there were cloudy days during the festival, the tree could be on all day and all night in a completely self-sustaining way. And as I drew up next to her, I didn't think Blaire had ever looked more beautiful than she did by Christmas tree light.

"How did things go in the community center?" she asked, by way of acknowledging my presence next to her.

"They went really well. You had practically the perfect number of volunteers, and they were all competent and able to help with every question or complaint. You might want to add an extra to allow bathroom and meal breaks on weekends and other high-volume times, but I was able to cover that tonight."

Blaire turned her head to look at me.

"That's a really good idea. I'll adjust the schedule as I can accordingly. Thanks for stepping up tonight. I'm a little surprised you're still here."

Even though the urge to see her practically propelled me to this spot, I found myself not quite ready to share what I had realized.

"I thought I would check in with you to see how things went, though I'm also surprised you're not passed out above Jitters by now."

Susie had lent Blaire the apartment above her shop anytime she needed it during the run of the festival, so she didn't have to go back and forth to her parent's "all the way across town" and save a whole five-minute commute. It was a sweet gesture, though, and a sign to how important Blaire was to this town.

Blaire turned her face back to look at the tree.

"I realized I hadn't really had a chance to just stop and look at the tree tonight, so I wanted to do that before I went to bed. Besides, I'm so wired from the adrenaline and excitement of the festival, I'm not sure I'd be able to sleep. I think tonight went really well; I just hope everything I did up to this point ends up being enough."

We let the silence sit between us for a few moments when I finally broached the photo I had just seen.

"Do you remember how I told you about the festival where the Holly Ridge kids basically ran me out of town?"

Blaire turned her whole body to face me this time.

"Yes, of course. Did it upset you that I vaguely referenced it in my welcome? I don't think anyone would ever have a chance of tying it back to you . . ."

"No, no, that's not where I'm headed with this. I don't think I ever told you about this girl, around my age at the time, that I noticed at the festival. She looked so happy to be there and was there with her mom and dad, and just looked so full of Christmas spirit and family love. I really wanted Christmas to be like that for me."

Blaire continued to look at me with empathy in her eyes, along with questions, wondering where I was heading with this. I turned my body, taking a step closer to Blaire at the same time, so our bodies were only separated by inches.

"This girl, in a red coat and shiny black boots, is something I thought about for years when I thought about Christmas and family. I always wondered what she grew up to be like, if she still loved Christmas, and still had that strong family connection."

Understanding dawned in Blaire's eyes now. After all, she had put together the history display and pulled together all the pictures, and it was her red coat and boots I was referencing.

"Turns out, she does still have all those things, but she also has so much more. She's funny and strong-willed, beautiful, and so organized. Her color coding makes my eyes cross, but she really just wants to share her compassion and love, which does happen to include an intense love of Christmas, with everyone."

I don't know whether it was the things my mom said to me a few nights before about second chances and making the family you choose, but I suddenly found, in the most cliché spot possible, in front of a blazing Christmas tree, that I wanted to choose Blaire tonight. I wanted to choose her for me. And I hoped she wanted to choose me too.

Chapter 24

Blaire

The night was an absolute blur. I checked in with so many visitors and townspeople, vendors and volunteers alike that I hadn't had a chance to stop and soak it all in. That's what I was doing when Cole found me—standing in front of the Christmas tree. It was here, my dream of planning my hometown festival was a reality, and the first night had gone so, so well.

A dream I didn't even know I had been harboring was playing out before me right now.

Cole was looking at me like he had been searching for something his whole life and had finally found it. Listening to him talk about how he had seen me and my parents all those years ago at the festival, it broke down the last line of defense around my heart. I realized he hadn't really needed to be around the past week or so, and definitely hadn't needed to be so helpful tonight, but he had done it anyway. And it seemed he had done it for me. That's something no man had ever done for me before, done something just because he knew it was important to me. Cole didn't want to take the credit or step onto the stage for any recognition in his role for the festival. He just wanted to support me.

With swells of romantic Christmas music playing inside my

head, I closed the distance between us, wrapping my hand around the back of his neck, and brought those plump, soft lips down where I could reach them. Cole let out a groan that I could only interpret as horny relief that zapped straight through my core and met my enthusiasm with passion of his own, reaching out to wrap one arm tightly around my waist and bury the other so deeply in my hair, I could feel his neatly trimmed nails digging into my scalp. At that point, he took control of the kiss, angling my head so it was just where he wanted it and demanding access to my mouth with his tongue. I let out a noise of my own that I didn't recognize and quickly realized we were headed to a place that could become indecent for public very quickly.

Slowly, I pulled back from the kiss, slowing his fervor with soft and gentle kisses. Our mouths parted, but I absolutely was not at all interested in separating our bodies from where they were touching. Because apparently, I was now living in a Hallmark film and it had started lightly snowing while we were lip locked, and I was just dumbfounded looking up at Cole's handsome face while the Christmas movie moment of my dreams occurred. Except, those movies always ended on a kiss, and I wasn't willing to have that be where our night ended.

Cole was looking back at me like he couldn't quite believe where he was right now, but this time, I wasn't worried about either or us bolting or running away.

"So, do you want to come back to my place? Well, the place I'm staying this week, which is above Jitters and definitely not in my childhood room in my parent's house. It smells like sugar."

Okay, even in the Hallmark movie of my life, this man still made me word-vomit.

Cole smiled down indulgently at me; a snowflake somehow landed on his eyelashes behind his glasses.

"I would love to come to your parent-free, bakery-scented place."

I entwined our gloved fingers and led the way across the square to Jitters, walking to the side alley that led to the apartment above the café. I led the way up the stairs, very aware that Cole was climbing closely behind me, and soon we would be alone again, but this time with very different intentions than the last time we were alone behind a locked door with a bed in the room.

I unlocked the door leading to the studio apartment. I had left a lamp by the bedside turned on, so the space was dimly lit, but cozy and inviting. It turns out that New England winters made for some very onerous outerwear to unburden yourself with before you could get *comfortable* with someone. A bit of a libido douser, if you will. I toed off my boots, unwound my scarf, and started to unzip my jacket, which led Cole to follow my lead. He had just pulled the beanie off his head, showing his hair to be a level midnight on the "just fucked" scale, and I hadn't even gotten my fingers in it yet.

I realized I was staring at him and felt the need to fill the quiet around us.

"Um, would you like something to drink? I have . . . well, water. And coffee."

Cole gave me a look that let me know he thought my question was ridiculous and unnecessary.

"I have no interest in putting my mouth on anything right now that isn't somehow attached to your body. Lips, breasts, skin, pussy. I want it all."

Well, alrighty then. Libido dialed back up to 100. That sort of descriptive talk created a direct impact on my panties, finding myself wet and aching for the mouth Cole had offered.

This girl isn't going to say no to that sort of offer made by the guy who's starred in her increasingly more specific fantasies when he was standing right in front of her, so I moved to push my arm out of my blazer sleeve.

"No, wait. I didn't get to undress you last time. And I have been dreaming about taking one of your blazers off you for months. Please, let me?"

Having lost the power of speech, I nodded as Cole approached me and guided me across the room toward the bed.

Keeping his eyes on mine, he gripped the lapel on each side of my blazer and pushed it slowly off my shoulders, letting his hands drag down the length of my arms until the jacket hit the floor. Still keeping his eyes firmly locked on mine, he gripped the bottom of my blouse, again keeping contact with my skin as he dragged his fingers up my sides, brushing the sides of my breasts and finally pulling the garment over the top of my head. I could feel my breathing pick up as my heart raced faster and wetness soaked my panties.

Cole's eyes darkened even more as he bent his head to leave a trail of kisses from the back of my ear, down my neck, licking the skin just above my collarbone. At this, I brought my arms up to grip his biceps to keep my balance, which had the bonus effect of pushing my tits closer to his mouth. Cole pulled first the right cup and then the left down under my breasts, presenting them to his waiting mouth, and proceeded to lavish each with attention, tightening my nipples into tight buds with his tongue and teeth one at a time. A husky moan left my lips at the sensations and while I never wanted him to stop what he was doing, I was also aching for him to touch me, lick me, fill me where I was aching.

Like the mind reader he was, Cole removed the suction from my left breast with an audible pop, and sank to his knees, so he was face-level with my waist. Chest heaving, I looked down at him, my hands now on his shoulders as he moved to unbutton my jeans, moving his hands around to cup my ass, while moving the denim down my legs.

"I love these panties, Blaire. I love the feeling of silk covering your ass, the sexiness of the lace, the sensibility of not having a string of floss between your cheeks all day. They're perfect for you."

Well, that was definitely the most detailed a man had ever been about my lingerie choices before, but that sort of thorough and interpretation of details was totally and completely Cole. Cole, who was now encouraging me to pick up one foot at a time so he could remove my jeans, while burying his nose into the damp silk of said lingerie. He inhaled deeply, saying, "My memory could never get your smell or your taste just right. You said this place would smell like sugar, but all I can smell is you."

Well shit. Apparently, the already awake sexy version of Cole is one who fires on all synapses and does not hold back when it comes to the dirty talk. I was not complaining.

He moved aside my underwear, running his finger through the wetness he found there. Just that one graze of a finger and I already felt like I was in danger of my knees buckling and falling to the ground. Sensing this, Cole put his hands on either side of my hips and gently pushed me backward, sending me bouncing slightly when my back hit the bed so suddenly. Pleased with the motion that move had done to my tits, Cole smirked and then went back to lavishing his attentions below my waist. Seeming to be done with my sensible panties, he pulled them down, waiting for me to tilt up my hips so he could peel them off.

I would have felt self-conscious, being fully bare on the bed with a man who was fully clothed, but no one had ever made me feel as safe or as sexy as Cole did in that moment. He pushed my knees wide apart and circled my clit with his pointer finger, making my hips shoot off the bed before he brought his other hand to my pelvis to hold it in place. Apparently, he was into making me feel my pleasure. He inserted first one finger and then two before curling them up to hit that spot deep inside of me, making me test the strength of that hand holding me in place. He brought his mouth to my clit at that point and moved his tongue and fingers in rhythm together, spiraling me higher and higher.

"Wait!" I exclaimed suddenly.

Cole immediately removed his hands and mouth, looking up at me with concern.

"No, I mean, that was fantastic. But I want you inside of me. Please?"

Cole suddenly looked furious at the world.

"I can't believe it, but again, I don't have a condom. I thought putting one in my wallet would just be too tempting."

"Well, I believe in learning from my mistakes. There are condoms in my backpack now, in the zipped pocket along the back. I wasn't sure if another blizzard would strike and trap you here during the festival, not able to get back across to your place . . . it was a whole fantasy thing."

Cole quickly moved to my bag, resting against the wall, and fished the three condoms I had stashed there when we got back from the capital two weeks ago.

Pulling off his shirt, again in that one-handed, behind-the-head sexy way, and throwing it on the floor, Cole made his way back to the bed, his eyes raking over my naked body like he couldn't wait to devour me whole.

Chapter 25

Cole

I stalked back to the bed, devouring Blaire's body with my eyes, thankful for the bedside lamp that was providing me more light to see her with than the moon had weeks ago when the power went out. I threw all three condoms onto the bedside table, along with my glasses, as I unbuttoned my pants and pulled them down, my long johns and briefs making their way to the floor shortly after. Blaire giggled at the sight of my long johns, but quickly sobered when my hard cock slapped against my stomach once I freed it from my briefs.

Her eyes were trained on my wrist as I gave myself a few quick pumps, twisting my wrist each time as I approached the head. *Three condoms,* I thought to myself, *three chances to bury myself inside her.*

Apparently impatient with my pace of standing over her and looking, Blaire started to skate her hand down her body to her beautiful, perfect pussy, playing with her clit as I stood there dumbfounded.

Let's focus on not blowing in the first condom within the first thirty seconds here, Thomas. Then we can worry about rounds two and three.

I climbed onto the bed and crawled over Blaire so her body was boxed under mine. I grabbed the hand that was playing with *my* pussy and brought her fingers to my mouth so I could taste her. Blaire's eyes widened as I sucked her fingers into my mouth, pulling them out with a pop and moving her arm so it was pinned above her head. For good measure, I grabbed her other hand and had it join the first, both fitting inside one of my hands.

"I'll be the one to stroke that pussy, thank you. It's owned me for the past two weeks. It's time I returned the favor."

As I brought my hand down to her slippery center, Blaire tilted her hips up to meet me, struggling to string a sentence together but managing to say, "I can appreciate where you're going with the whole arms pinned above the head thing, but one of us going to need two hands to put that condom on because I thought I asked you to get inside me a good five minutes ago."

I really met my match with this one. She accepted my dirty talk and urges to be in charge in the bedroom, but also wasn't afraid to let me know when something wasn't working for her. I released her hands and handed her the condom, moving back so she could sit up and roll it down my cock, but not before working the drops of precum gathered on the tip of cock back into my skin with a few pumps of her own. My hand never left Blaire's clit during her sure-handed maneuvering, but the few additional pumps she added to my cock after it was sheathed in latex was enough to have me laying her back on the bed and pinning her arms above her head again.

"That's enough of that, ma'am. Now that I'm ready, I can't go another second without being inside you."

I brought my other hand to the base of my cock and lined myself up with Blaire's center, the tip brushing her tantalizing pink flesh. I couldn't decide where to look, at Blaire's face to watch her gasp when she felt that first brush of contact, or down where we were about to be joined. Eventually, the joining won out, and I watched as I inched myself inside of her until I was fully seated inside her, locking together like a perfect fit.

Now I looked up to see her eyes searching for mine, her chest heaving in tempo with my own, both of us struggling with the effort to stay still. I decided to release her wrists at the same time she pushed against my grip to move her arms to the back of my neck.

"Move, please," she said as she pulled my head down to crush my lips to hers, and I had no choice but to comply with her request. I slowly drew myself back and thrust back in, this time meeting Blaire's hips in a thrust of her own. We fell into a slow and steady rhythm with our mouths and our hips, until she slid her hands from my neck down to my ass and said, "Harder, faster," against my mouth. It was like she was in touch with my base desires, and I instantly picked up the pace, pistoning into her faster and harder while her legs replaced her hands above my ass, changing the angle and causing me to go deeper.

I could tell Blaire was getting closer to the precipice with every thrust, but unfortunately, so was I, and I absolutely could not finish before I got her there. I started naming Santa's reindeer and the gifts from the Twelve Days of Christmas in my head, anything to stave off the tingling that was growing at the base of my spine. Then I felt Blaire's core tighten around my cock as she threw her head back and yelled, "Oh, Cole!" her orgasm overtaking her. I slid her left leg up from my waist to my shoulder, allowing me to go even deeper still and prolong her orgasm as I finally allowed the tingling to overtake me and unloaded inside the condom with one final thrust.

Releasing her leg, I did everything I could to hold most of my body weight off her while I caught my breath and the full power of my vision returned. I brushed some hair off Blaire's face that was stuck with sweat and couldn't believe this gorgeous, fantastic girl had allowed me the privilege of watching her, joining her, while we lost control.

I eased out of her, pressing a kiss on her forehead, saying, "I'll be right back."

I walked quickly to the bathroom, disposed of the condom, and wet a washcloth I found on the towel rack with warm water in the sink. I walked back to Blaire and used it to clean her so she would be more comfortable, before climbing into bed next to her and gathering her so her head was on my chest. Blaire's hand stroked up and down my side in a relaxing, comforting rhythm.

"Thank you for listening when I gave instructions, Cole."

I chuckled, aware that she would feel the rumbling of my laugh against her cheek. Was it just an hour ago we were standing out by the tree, with me hoping she would choose me? I felt incredibly chosen at the moment.

"Thank you for the invitation, Blaire."

Saturday morning dawned bright and clear, the type of morning that was misleading in the wintertime, because it made it look like it would feel much warmer outside than it actually was. I should feel bad about how little sleep I had allowed Blaire to get, but I had also woken up with my cock in her mouth and she was the one who suggested getting a shower at 4:00 a.m., so I think we were both equally to blame for our sleeplessness.

I woke up before her this morning, our legs tangled together underneath the blankets and sheets, facing each other, so I had a chance to look at her. I had seen so many sides of this woman by this point—angry, frustrated, sassy, passionate, excited—but this was the first time I had really seen her at rest. She was always gorgeous, but knowing that I was seeing this side of her because she invited me to do so did something to my chest.

Blaire started to stir, her eyes blinking slowly and bringing her hand up to touch her use-swollen and darkened lips, like she needed to remind herself last night was real.

"Morning," I said to her, not able to keep the smile off my face.

"Good morning," she replied, her face breaking into a matching smile that seemed to light up the whole room with her joy.

"Sorry today is going to be such a long day for you on limited sleep."

"No, you're not," she replied, her eyes sparkling with laughter.

Flashes of Blaire riding me, her head thrown back as her orgasm hit her, flashed through my memory.

"No, I'm not," I responded, feeling my smile morph into what I believe a romance author would describe as wicked.

"I do need to get up and get going though, The Holly Ridge Theater's run of *A Christmas Carol* starts with a matinee today, and Santa will be setting up in the gazebo, so there are sure to be things that will need my attention. And I'm sure you want to get out of here before all the stall vendors start to show up. I doubt you'll sneak past Susie, but she's loyal. She won't say anything to anyone else."

A look of hurt and confusion must have crossed over my face —she was ashamed for me to be seen leaving here?

"Oh, no! Cole!" Blaire exclaimed, placing her hand on my face, immediately interpreting my expression correctly. "I'm thinking only of making sure no one sees you leave so it doesn't get back to the state audit office, you know, your new bosses, that you were seen leaving my 'quarters' in the early morning hours. Plus, I already ruffled enough feathers with my inference that Holly Ridge wasn't always entirely welcoming with their festivals in the past. I don't need them to turn on me completely while the festival is just getting started."

I wasn't 100 percent sure the second part of her statement actually made me feel better, but she had a point about the rules laid out by the audit office. And then Blaire removed her hand from my face and sat up, stretching, causing the sheet to fall to her waist and bare her perfect tits to the morning light, and any worries or hurt I felt went by the wayside.

Blaire laughed at my laser focus as she pulled the sheet back up, covering up my early morning delight.

"There's no time, Cole. Get moving."

Huffing, I pulled back the sheet and stood, searching for my boxer briefs on the ground in all the clothing carnage from last night. I stepped into them and turned around to find Blaire gripping the sheet tightly against her chest, staring at where my bare ass had been moments ago.

"There's no time, Blaire. Get moving."

She rolled her eyes at me good-naturedly, and we both moved in an easy, comfortable rhythm around each other in the small space, her getting ready for the day and me getting ready to head back to Winterberry Glen, alone.

"Well, I'll probably come back later to check on how things are going . . ."

Blaire met me at the door, pulling my hat out of my hands and placing it on my head, making sure to cover my ears.

"I would love it if you came back later today. Let me know when you want to see the production at the theater. I can set aside a ticket, or two, if your mom would want to come as well."

She pressed a quick kiss to my lips, pulling back but lingering close to my face, checking to see if it was okay that she had invited my mom to something.

"I'll do that. She may want to bring her new beau instead of me, in fact. We're decorating her new Christmas tree today, so I'll check in with her then."

"A tree?!"

I smiled down at her enthusiasm over me having some decorations in my life.

"It's something she wanted to do this year, and I have a hard time telling that woman no. I'll show you pictures the next time I see you."

"It's a date."

With that, I opened the door and made my way down the stairs, failing to avoid peeking in the window of Jitters as I walked by, so I caught Susie noticing my origin and breaking into a wide grin as she set about preparing her bakery case for the day. I lifted my hand in a wave and kept on walking back to the parking area where I left my car overnight.

I was sure there was a chill in the air, it being mid-December in New England, but I sure couldn't feel it.

Chapter 26

December 20

Cole

Blaire and I fell into a pattern after the opening night of the festival. I would come to Holly Ridge under the guise of being helpful with the festival, but really, I couldn't make myself stay away from Blaire. We usually ended up back at her borrowed studio above Jitters. I found out the third night that Susie had left her a key to Jitters for "emergencies" and made her break in to "borrow" a bit of cookie icing that I proceeded to use to decorate and then lick off Blaire's body like my own personal Christmas cookie decorating contest.

Blaire mentioned her muscles were a bit sore from overuse, which led me to mention I had a bathtub with Jacuzzi jets in it, which inspired us to spend last night at my place for the first time. Having Blaire wet and naked in my tub, with me holding her legs open in front of one of the Jacuzzi jets while I directed her to play with her tits? That was my own personal Christmas miracle. Having her flip the script on me and suck me off while a jet massaged my taint would keep me going through the new year.

I found myself not minding the Christmas music or corny romantic Christmas movies Blaire would put on in the background while we were spending time snuggled together in her bed or mine. I don't know if it was just exposure therapy or if my Christmas spirit was slowly being reignited by this magical girl, but it was the best December and lead-up to Christmas I had ever had.

It was after the night in my tub, Blaire had just left to get back to Holly Ridge to oversee a final run-through ahead of the Christmas parade, that reality finally came calling, literally.

I had just gotten out of the shower when I heard my phone ringing in my bedroom. I walked into the room with just a towel around my waist, picking up the phone to see "State Audit Office" showing up on the caller ID. Running my hand through my damp hair, I took a deep breath and answered.

"This is Cole Thomas."

"Hi Cole. Barney Windfall here. How are you doing this morning?"

"Hi Mr. Windfall. I'm doing all right. How about yourself?"

"Can't complain. Just a few more days until the office closes for the holidays. Listen, I wanted to give you a call to update you about the status of the Holly Ridge festival and confirm your start date with us when you come aboard next year."

I felt my knees bending as I sat down on the edge of my bed. Next year. As in just a few weeks. And I could tell from his voice that the news about Holly Ridge would be something I'd want to be sitting down for.

"We've been looking over the numbers Holly Ridge's City Council's office is sending over each morning, and while you did a fantastic job keeping the budget in check and offsetting expenses with some of these sponsorships, I'm afraid unless something drastically changes over the next ten days of the festival, it's still not going to be enough to save the town."

Six months ago, hell even three months ago, I could have imagined myself feeling smug at the news of Holly Ridge being absorbed by Winterberry Glen. But somehow, now that the news was tied up with a big Greene ribbon in my mind, all I could feel was a sinking feeling in my stomach.

"Well, that's too bad to hear . . . I know Miss Greene, and well, I mean the whole town, worked incredibly hard on this year's festival."

"That's just how these things go sometimes, my boy," Barney replied. "But as you'll remember, we were interested in your work overseeing the budget and maintaining a professional relationship in tense scenarios like these. They'll be more common than you think and will certainly crop-up in your work at the state level, and we cannot have been more impressed with your work."

"Well, thank you, sir," I answered, almost on autopilot, my mind trying to catch up with the news. Suddenly, I had an idea.

"And by the way, sir, I had nothing to do with securing those sponsorships. That was entirely Blaire Greene's doing. It was a pleasure to manage her throughout this process. She's really a very talented festival planner."

"Is that so?" Barney replied, seeming to take the bait. "My wife works in the special events department here at the state house and was certainly impressed at all the sponsorships in a budget like this festival's, especially after the budget was such a disaster in years past. Should Miss Greene be interested in her next move, now that it appears Holly Ridge will no longer have a Christmas festival to plan, I'd be happy to make a connection."

Remembering who I was talking to, and his allusion to professional relationships moments earlier, I didn't want to lay it on too thick.

"I'm not sure what will be next for Ms. Greene, but should an opportunity arise for me to bring this up, I most certainly will do so."

"All right, Cole, well, I won't keep you much longer. Will a start date of January fifth work for you? Give a bit of time to get settled in after the start of the year and then hit the ground running?"

Just a little over two weeks away. Because of course, in the eyes of Barney and everyone else in the state audit office, after securing the job three weeks ago, I would have spent the last three weeks securing housing in the capital and packing and such, not obsessing over the festival planner I wasn't supposed to be having a personal relationship with.

"Of course, Mr. Windfall, that sounds perfect. I appreciate the generosity of the buffer," I heard myself saying. Wow, my autopilot mouth was good.

"Very well, son. Have a very Merry Christmas and a Happy New Year. We look forward to having you as part of the team."

"Thank you, sir. Same to you and yours."

I hung up the phone and took in my sparsely decorated bedroom, that suddenly seemed to have lost the brightness Blaire left in it just an hour or so ago. This was what I wanted all along. This is what I had been working toward. Holly Ridge had been run into the ground by their City Council, and it wasn't Blaire's fault she couldn't save them. I would go to the state capital and start over there. Maybe Blaire would want to come along and work on state initiatives in the special events office. But if not, we had only been doing whatever it was we were doing for a whole five days now. It would be unfortunate to leave her behind, but it would be worth it for the pursuit of my goals. That's what mattered now. Holly Ridge was in the past and maybe Blaire Greene would need to stay there too.

Chapter 27

Blaire

Was it possible that just this morning I woke up in Cole's bed, my legs tangled in his, watching his eyes do that sleepy-blink-awake thing, while a slow smile curled his lips when my face came into focus? That had to be a scene from someone else's life, because right now, nothing in my life was anywhere near that good.

To say the final parade run through this afternoon had gone about as smoothly as a house full of fifteen people trying to catch an international flight that leaves in forty-five minutes would be putting it mildly.

Half of the high school marching band had come down with food poisoning from a chili-cook off fundraiser they held yesterday, so their Christmas carols left a little to be desired. Frosty's winter wonderland float had somehow gotten wet and turned all the "snow" decorations yellow. The candy cane marshals couldn't find their canes and the truck that was supposed to pull Santa's sleigh got a flat tire mid-route. And, somehow, out of a 34th Street-fueled nightmare, Santa himself was hungover and had to lean over the edge of the sleigh to avoid adding his own chunky decorations to the scene, definitely scarring the dance class that was letting out of Lydia's dance studio at that exact moment.

"All right, everyone!"

I addressed the crowd of parade participants gathered around the end of the parade route.

"That may not have been the best run-through in the world, but it definitely gives us room to create some parade magic this evening when it's time for the real thing! Joe, try to find some fake snow spray over at the general store to turn Frosty's snow white-ish again. Hopefully the dark night will help cover up the yellow hue as well. Marchers, maybe let's pick one song to play up and down the parade route and really nail the thing. And for the love of Kris Kringle, can someone please get Santa a greasy sandwich, some coffee, and a water?"

I noted that my voice got higher and the speech faster with each suggestion I rattled off. I took a deep breath and put what I hoped was a reassuring smile on my face.

"Okay, everyone, thanks so much for joining in the parade. I'll see you back at the starting point in two hours."

After addressing some more individual concerns from the participants, locating some large plastic candy canes in the bushes surrounding the gazebo and checking to be sure the cars that had been still parked along the parade route during rehearsal had all moved out of the way, it was forty-five minutes to the parade kick off. Holly Ridgeians and out-of-towners alike were lining the streets, bundled up against the evening cold, some having brought blankets to tuck around their legs while seated in their camping chairs and on the curb.

Everything has gone so smoothly up to this point, Blaire. There's always going to be one hiccup in a festival. Hopefully, this is Holly Ridge's, I thought to myself, now that I finally had time to breathe. I searched the crowd for Cole's broad-shouldered figure while checking my phone to see if I missed a text from him. This morning he mentioned he had a few things to do during the day but would be sure to come over in time for the parade kick off. I found myself wanting to find him in the crowd, seeking his steady and calming presence to soothe the jitteriness I felt after such a rough afternoon. Somehow, I knew he would make me feel better, even if he couldn't give me the hug I was so deeply craved while we were out in public.

My eyes traveled over the crowd, but I didn't see that familiar head of brown hair and sparkling brown eyes behind glasses and my phone hadn't suddenly displayed any messages, so I decided to run up to the studio above Jitters for an extra pair of gloves before I got sucked back into any festival prep. If Susie saw me through the window heading up the stairs and waved me in for a Peppermint Mocha on my way back down, well, that definitely wouldn't make me feel worse.

I rounded the corner to the alley next to Jitters and suddenly jumped back to the front of the building. Two people were sitting on the staircase leading up to the apartment—Cole and Tanya.

Shit. What is Tanya doing here tonight? I hope she wasn't around for any part of that rehearsal. And why is she talking to Cole?

I could hear their voices rumbling, so apparently they hadn't spotted me before I darted out of sight. Gloves completely forgotten, I peeked around the corner, using the crack between the wall and a very conveniently placed drainpipe to take a closer look. Tanya had her phone out and appeared to be recording their conversation. Poking my head around the corner allowed me to just make out their conversation, the noise from the street behind me almost loud enough that it would drown out their voices if the wind changed direction.

"Thanks, Cole, this has all been really helpful. So, for one last question, on the record, do you think the Christmas festival is going to save Holly Ridge?"

Cole paused, a pained look on his face I had never seen before taking over his features.

"As a financial guy, I understand why the state did what it did. Holly Ridge was in trouble and needed some intervention. They have the best interests of the fiscal health of the area and the state in mind. As a citizen experiencing the Christmas festival with new eyes and a new perspective after growing up in the area? I think it was a huge burden to take on, and if nothing else, the former mayor's daughter gave her town one hell of a festival to hang their hats on if it should be the last one. Blaire Greene—"

The fire station siren went off at that moment, signaling that there were only fifteen minutes until the parade started, and also drowning out the rest of Cole's statement. I think I had heard enough though. It sure didn't seem like Cole believed I could do this, and I absolutely hated the term "former mayor's daughter" coming out of his mouth. Yet, I was still frozen in place and once the whistle stopped, I heard Tanya ask, "And off the record?"

Cole sighed. "Off the record? It's not going to happen. The money brought in so far doesn't indicate that Holly Ridge is going to earn what they need to keep the town charter in to next year."

At this moment, a cacophony of jingle bells went off behind me, causing me to jump and turn around. Phil was handing out the jingle bells we had ordered to help kids in attendance at the parade welcome Santa down the street and had just reached the Jitters' block. Of course, the kids weren't going to wait until they could see Santa to give their bells a test run.

I couldn't believe it. When had Cole found out the money wasn't going to be enough? Why was he telling Tanya, but not me? Him not believing in me made a bit more sense now, because it seemed like I had failed. I wasn't in charge of sending the official reporting to the state capitol, that responsibility was with the City Council's office, but I was providing those numbers to the council and thought that we were doing really well—better than the projections we had set out that would have us meet our goal.

The continued jingling from the bells finally saturated my brain, and I realized where I was. Money threshold met or not, there were a ton of people here waiting for a parade. I started jogging up the sidewalk, dodging parents carrying toddlers on their shoulders and teenagers trying to look like they were too cool for a Christmas parade. My meltdown would have to wait until later. It was time to have a parade.

Cole

It felt good to get the news off my chest that it didn't look like the festival was going to bring in enough money to save Holly Ridge. Tanya had become something of a colleague after our initial meeting over the summer, calling me the day after our lunch and walk around the town square to apologize for her behavior. It turns out that Christmas was somewhat of a sore spot for her as well, and she had lost control of herself that day. She asked me about financial implications related to her different articles and focuses, anonymously and off the record, so I knew I could trust her to keep the news between us. I strongly suggested she come back to Holly Ridge during the festival to follow-up with her article from over the summer during one of our e-mail exchanges and I was happy to see she had taken the hint.

Bells jingling in the background, Tanya let her shoulders slump, leaning against the side railing of the steps leading up to Blaire's temporary studio apartment, her professional facade cracking slightly.

"Well, damn it. I was really rooting for you guys—the small-town charm, town feud, the dynamic between you and Blaire, it really spoke to me, and I was hoping she would be able to pull it off."

"Yeah, I'm not looking forward to breaking the news to her, but I wouldn't want her to hear from the City Council or anyone else. I feel like they wouldn't handle it well."

Tanya looked at me slyly. "I'm sure you could come up with a way to soften the blow."

I swallowed a laugh. That's the other reason Tanya and I were able to be collegial. She had picked up on the flirty, jealous vibes between Blaire and I, and while of course I had confirmed nothing, Tanya really was too good of a journalist to miss what apparently Blaire and I weren't too good at hiding if you looked long and hard enough.

Tanya let out a soft laugh, shaking her head at my taciturn response.

"Well, looks like the parade is going to be starting any minute, if the volume of jingle bells is any indication. This is the last time I'll probably make it to Holly Ridge this year. Are you sure I can't convince you to blow off the state suits and come work for me?"

Tanya had managed to secure a streaming service show, so needed to bring on a full-time accountant to manage all her business ventures. She had been trying to convince me to take the gig over the last several weeks.

"I'm sure. I've been working toward this job at the capital for too long. It's my next step."

Tanya nodded and got up, her mauve-heeled, knee-high boots matching the shade of her long pea coat perfectly. She put her phone in her large handbag and secured it safely over her shoulder, ready to head out to the street to join the festivities.

"You know, Cole, just because it's the way it's always been, doesn't mean it's the way it has to be. Thanks for the chat. When you're able to send me official confirmation on the financial status of Holly Ridge, will you let me know? I'll see you around."

With that, she disappeared into the crowd of people, leaving me in the shadows next to Jitters. Cryptic one-liners hadn't been Tanya's style in the short time I knew her, but in this case, she was wrong. It was time to keep moving on and leave the past behind me.

I pulled my phone out of my messenger bag, realizing I hadn't had a chance to check in with Blaire to see how the rehearsal went and how she was feeling headed into the parade. It disappointed me to not see a text waiting from her, but also understood as someone who had gotten caught up in his work a time or two myself. Typing out a message, I pushed to my feet and made my way to the sidewalk, hoping to use my height to my advantage to get a view of the floats and local celebrities as they passed by the town square.

Cole (7:03 p.m.): Hey B. Hope everything went off without a hitch today. I'm ready for a jolly old parade.
Blaire (7:05 p.m.): Hitches were had. But it's fine.

I frowned at my screen. I hoped nothing too terrible had gone wrong today. I could have helped out if she needed me to. And there was that word again—*fine*—it never meant what the dictionary alluded it did.

Cole (7:07 p.m.): I'm sorry it wasn't a smooth sailing day. Good sized crowd though! Hopefully they all head over to the market after the parade is done.

I held my phone in my hand, waiting for a buzz for her return message. Nothing came for a few minutes as I watched parade goers receive candy from teenagers in red and white striped outfits holding large plastic candy canes. Well, she was at the start of the parade, I'm sure she was busy.

Cole (7:25 p.m.): Do you want to come back over to my place tonight and take another soak in the tub? I promise it can be as relaxing or stimulating as you want it to be. Your lead. I'm just sorry I wasn't around for the hitches and would like to see you.

Still nothing. I could see the Frosty float on the opposite side of the square, which I remembered was the last float before Santa himself appeared past the grandstand. I thought about dipping into Jitters to grab both of us a coffee, for after the parade was over, planning to head toward the starting point and hope my path would cross with Blaire's when my hand buzzed.

Blaire (7:32 p.m.): I have a migraine, and my mom wants me home to consult on some last-minute present options. I think I'm out for tonight.

I felt a pit of disappointment in my stomach. It may have only been less than a week, but I had gotten used to seeing Blaire at the end of each day. Sure, the sex was a great bonus, but I meant it when I told her I just wanted to help her relax after a rough day. Sleeping without her was going to be cold and lonely tonight.

Cole (7:33 p.m.): Sorry about your head, B. Hope your mom takes it easy on you and you can get some good sleep. Let me know when you want me back here to help?

We always made plans for the next day and how I would help while we were together in bed, so I felt a bit adrift without knowing where Blaire needed me next. I would just have to trust she would let me know.

I stared at the screen and saw the dots appear, showing Blaire was typing something, and I waited in anticipation, just to see them disappear again.

I looked up and saw Santa crossing through the grandstand of the parade, looking a little green around the edges, but waving to the crowd.

I know how you feel, buddy.

I turned and walked down the sidewalk to the event parking lot where I had left my car earlier that evening, envisioning a very different ending to this day. *I would just have to check in with Blaire in the morning to see how I could help*, I told myself. I could use the evening to do some packing or even catch up on sleep, since I hoped I would be sleeping, and also not sleeping, with Blaire again tomorrow night.

Chapter 28

December 23

Blaire

Things with the festival had gotten back on track after the disastrous parade rehearsal. Even the actual parade itself went better than I expected after the train wreck I watched earlier that afternoon. It was me who was still feeling off the rails. I wasn't even excited about rotating through my Christmas dresses underneath my blazers—I had more than enough to make it through the last week of the festival—I just reached into my closet at home at random for whatever dress was next in the row.

Yes, I was back to staying at my parent's house every night. I really did feel like I needed to check in on presents with my mom when I told Cole that three days ago and my head did feel like it was going to explode after what I had overheard Cole and Tanya talking about, but I could have made it back to the Jitters' loft that night if I needed to. I can admit I was hiding. I was hiding from Cole, but I was also hiding from the town, so I didn't spill the news that I had failed them. I was honestly even hiding from my parents in their own home, so they didn't look too closely into my eyes and read the news.

It's not that Cole hadn't reached out. I could sense his hurt and confusion, even through his texts. The day after the parade, I hid away from the town square at the start of the house decorating route—cars could pay $5 a head or bring one non-perishable item per person to go through the official route after dark. It was our charitable portion of the festival—but I heard from Susie he was in Jitters asking about me. He only reached out twice yesterday, and as far as I knew, hadn't come by the festival at all. There was nothing from him yet today. I hated that even though I was intentionally avoiding him, I still wanted to hear from him, just so I could choose to ignore him.

I was lost in thought, walking through the town square, heading to check on the ornament auction set to take place from the gazebo in the next hour, when my phone started buzzing in my pocket. Fishing it out of my jacket, I saw Susie's name appear on the home screen.

"Hey Susie, what's up?"

"Hey Blaire, sorry to bug you, I know you're swamped, but I hear a weird sort of pipe-clanking noise coming from up in the studio. Do you mind going by to check it out?"

I stopped in my tracks, turning to face Jitters. I may have been avoiding the studio because it was draped in memories of Cole and I tangled up together, both during the sexy times and during the sweet times where we were just talking or making our way through my yearly Christmas movie list, so I wasn't thrilled about the idea of going up there, even for Susie.

"Are you not in the shop? I'm about ready to go—"

"Oh no, I'm here, but I can't seem to find my key, and you have my extra. I know it's a lot to ask, but I would just hate for the water heater to burst and flood the shop during the last few days before Christmas. I have all of my holiday meal desserts to finish up that people have been ordering for weeks."

Damn, Susie was laying it on thick today.

"Okay, sure. I'm in the square now. I'll be right over."

"Thanks so much Blaire. I'll have a mocha waiting for you when you're done. Talk to you soon!"

Sighing, knowing that I would do pretty much anything for the woman who kept me caffeinated, I tucked my phone back into my pocket and started walking toward the alley. Hopefully, it would be just a quick fix, like turning off the radiator or something, and I could be in and out in just a second.

I walked up the stairs, hearing the echoes of Cole telling Tanya he didn't believe in me and stopped at the door to fish out my key.

That's weird. You would think if Susie could hear the clanking from inside Jitters, I would be able to hear it standing outside the door to the apartment, I thought to myself as I turned the key and twisted the handle to push the door open.

I stepped inside, scanning the room from right to left, when out of the corner of my eye, I saw movement.

"Fucking jingle bells!" I yelled on instinct, before taking in the familiar figure and realizing it was Cole standing in the kitchenette, leaning against the counter.

With my hand to my chest, I waited for my heart rate to slow down while I eyed that handsome brown-haired man, daring to stand there with his glasses on and shirt sleeves rolled up to show off his forearms. I looked beside him and yup, on the counter, there was that messenger bag.

"What are you doing here, Cole?"

"I like the candy canes today. They look good with the red blazer. Though the sleigh print from the day before last was pretty cute. What was on yesterday's dress? I couldn't tell."

I blinked at him.

"Santa Clauses," I responded warily. Why were we talking about my dresses? And did that mean he had been at the festival yesterday and had managed to find me the day before?

"What are you doing here, Cole?" I repeated.

"Well, I figured when you volunteered to sit at the collection station for the house tour after not returning my texts all day, when you told me a few weeks ago that's where you stuck your least favorite volunteers because it was so boring, that meant you needed some space. And then yesterday, you were painting faces at the children's festival, basically ensuring small people surrounded you all day, so we wouldn't be able to get a moment alone without causing suspicion. But today was one too many days without you talking to me, so I may have convinced Susie to lure you here so we could talk."

I continued to blink at Cole, amazed that he had slipped past my radar the past few days after being so in tune to his whereabouts for the week—okay, months—prior.

I was not having this conversation with him. I wasn't ready, and I didn't like the fact that he had used Susie and my peppermint mochas to trick me.

I eyed the door, trying to figure out if I could just walk out, now that it was apparent there was no pipe problem at all going on.

Cole apparently tracked my eye movement and figured out my plan, because he responded, "Go ahead. Try it, Blaire, and I will pick you up, pin you on that bed and we will have this conversation with me holding you down, so you have to talk to me."

That got my nipples excited, those traitorous, nerve-filled buds. Down, girls, we are not thinking about him pinning us anywhere. We do not feel warm, fluttering, sexual feelings for men who think we are nothing more than our father's connections and aren't capable of succeeding.

I turned to walk to the table to sit down, figuring staying far away from that bed was in my best interests. With my back to Cole, I asked, "How did you get Susie to help you, anyway? You're from Winterberry Glen."

I turned around to see Cole try to hide his flinch. *Maybe a smidge too harsh, B.*

"Well, I guess Susie doesn't actually buy too much into the feud. Or maybe it helps that I was in there every day over the past two weeks buying us food and drinks, and we chatted a few times. And the fact that she definitely caught me sneaking back to my car a few mornings definitely doesn't hurt."

I felt my cheeks warm at the thought of Susie, who's known

me my whole life, catching a boy sneaking out of the apartment she's lending me. Hopefully her reputation for town gossip steel trap still holds true.

I straightened my dress and crossed one leg over the other, not missing how Cole's eyes went to the hem as it rose higher on my thighs as he crossed the room to join me. Good lord, man, it had only been three days and I'm wearing leggings.

Cole crossed his arms on the table and my eyes zeroed in on his forearms again. Okay, fine, I take back judging him for the leg looking.

Suddenly, I couldn't hold it back anymore.

"Why didn't you tell me that the festival wasn't going to make enough money to save Holly Ridge?"

Whatever Cole expected me to say first, it was not that. His face wore a look of complete shock.

"Where did you hear that?"

"I heard you and Tanya talking about it the night of the parade. How could you tell her first?"

I didn't love that I was forced to admit to eavesdropping quite so quickly, but it turned out that among the hurt of failure and the fact that Cole didn't believe in me, there was also the fact that he had told Tanya before he told me.

"Blaire, I would have told you later that night. I found out that morning after you left. I had no idea you were around when Tanya and I were talking. I never would have wanted you to find out that way."

"Well, I did, and that sucked. Why would you tell her, anyway? She's a reporter, she's totally going to break the story before the festival is over and ruin the remaining days of Holly Ridge and the town's Christmas."

"I promise she won't print it, Blaire. I trust her. We've talked about off-the-record things before and she never—"

"Oh, so you've just been feeding her information about Holly Ridge this whole time?"

"The only time we talked about Holly Ridge was that day this summer when you were there and three days ago. Tanya's been asking me financial questions about other small-town matters, and I've been answering them off the record, so she can go digging in the right direction. It would be a conflict of interest to do it otherwise. She even wants . . . well, it doesn't matter what she wants. This is about you and me and how it feels that you've been avoiding me for three days!"

It definitely matters about what Tanya wants, but my brain got stuck on the fact that he wanted to talk about how something feels.

"You, Cole Thomas, avoider extraordinaire, who made us meet virtually after an *almost*-kiss, want to sit here and talk about feelings? In person? Isn't it your turn to run away? Sure you wouldn't rather do that?"

Cole

No, I didn't really *want* to talk about feelings, but I was sitting here in this small apartment, looking at how pretty Blaire looked in her dress and blazer and remembering how good she smelled, and I realized how I felt after she had avoided me for three days was really, really shitty. And it was time to talk about it.

I wiped my hand over my face, buying a second to collect myself.

"Look, Blaire, I'm sorry you found out that the numbers aren't looking positive the way you did, but I still don't understand why you didn't just ask me about it. We could have fought. You used to love fighting with me!"

She bit her bottom lip and looked away from me, showing a vulnerable side I had only seen a few times before.

"It's not just that. It's that you also don't believe that I would be capable of doing this, and that I'm only here because I'm my father's daughter. After everything I've told you about how I feel like I don't measure up to my family, and this was my chance, I think I could have been okay with the festival not making enough money if I felt like people, like you, believed that I deserved the chance to try."

I was stunned. Blaire thought I didn't believe in her? What conversation had she been listening to between Tanya and me?

Rather than waste time trying to replay our conversation in my head, I decided to play my ace in the hole instead.

"I don't believe in you? I would never say that. If that's the case, why have I been talking to my bosses at the state capital about getting you a job with their special events department?"

The ice in Blaire's eyes when she turned back to look at me was far colder than any temperatures the New England winter had reached this far.

"Why in the world would I want to plan festivals for the state? Especially whenever someone else, another man, made the connection to get me an in with the department? All I ever wanted was to move back here, back home, and work on *this* Christmas festival. Meet a nice guy who would believe in me and support me. Have a marriage that was as close to perfect as my sister's or my parent's. Maybe have some kids and raise our family here, going to the same festival that I went to. That's all I ever wanted. You don't want to do any of that, do you?"

I sat back in my chair, stunned. Somehow in the buzz of the festival, the spirit of Blaire's Christmas cheer, and the warmth of the bedsheets, I had forgotten at the root just how incompatible Blaire and I were.

The ice in Blaire's eyes started to melt, and I opened my mouth to say something, anything, to try to salvage this.

Blaire shook her head.

"Cole, you're leaving in just a matter of days. So, start the leaving now and go."

I couldn't find anything in myself to argue with that. I stood slowly, my eyes locked on hers as I took a step toward Blaire and bent at the waist to place a kiss on the crown of her head, pausing with my eyes closed to allow my other senses to take over, to feel the softness of her hair against my cheek, to inhale her scent deep into my lungs, to hear her breath hitch as she leaned forward to rest her head against my chest.

Finally, I made myself pull back and walked to the counter to grab my coat and messenger bag. I paused at the door to look back over my shoulder, who wiped her eyes quickly when she saw my movement. She raised her hand in a wave and I nodded in response, before pulling the door shut and making my way down those stairs one final time.

I peaked in the window of Jitters, knowing Susie would be on alert to see when and who came out of the apartment first. I offered her a wave of thanks, but apparently my face betrayed not all had gone well, as Susie's hopeful face fell, and she crossed her arms at her chest, giving me a sympathetic nod before I continued walking back to my car, back to Winterberry Glen, back to my boxes, and back to my predetermined life.

Chapter 29

Christmas Eve

   Cole

I now knew first-hand the meaning of the phrase "very slowly, then all at once." That was the best way to describe the impact Blaire had on my life. I had spent so much time with my walls up, trying to ignore the way she made me feel when she was around, but once I had given in, my world had changed all at once. And then again, after our "mutual ending," it turned out my world changed in an instant. I should have been able to shake it off and get back to packing and preparing for my move, but I found myself sitting in place, staring at the wall, some belonging or another in my hand, open and mostly empty boxes surrounding me.

The last thing I felt like doing tonight was having Christmas Eve dinner, but my mom insisted that this would be the most magical evening for me to meet her new manfriend—I refused to even think the term boyfriend in relation to my mother—Tom, so here I was, sitting in my childhood living room, which was all decked out in holiday spirit, while Christmas classics played from the speaker on the mantel.

That was another thing that had changed slowly and then all

at once—my mom had been working on herself in silence for so long that I hadn't noticed the changes, but now that she'd let me in on her secret, it was like she was a completely different woman. Yes, she was still the loving Italian woman who would call me on my shit and make sure my plate was never empty until I was literally bursting, but she was also lighter and freer somehow. I think Tom had a lot to do with that.

I was sitting in a different chair, still staring at the wall, nursing a Christmas Ale, the cheer even having taken over our alcohol choices, when Mom came into the living room from the kitchen.

"Tom's finishing up on the last of the seven fishes, so we should be ready to eat soon. I tried to tell the man we've never eaten the feast of seven fishes on Christmas Eve before and we'd be okay not doing so now, but he insisted."

The swoony look in Mom's eye told me how happy she was to have someone make an extreme effort in something, even after she had told him not to. That's absolutely what she deserved and it made me feel a bit better about leaving her behind, knowing Tom would be here—but hopefully not here, in this house, all the time, here—when I was gone.

"That sounds great, Mom. The smells are . . . interesting, but I'm sure it'll all be delicious."

"While we have a few minutes, why don't you tell me why you're sitting out here looking like a lump of coal instead of *my* Cole? Ready to move to the big city and take on a new adventure?"

"Wow, Mom, real original, never heard that one before."

I had actually heard that one before. I was pretty sure it was one of the Christmas-themed insults Blaire lobbed at me last spring. I took another swig of beer to try to hide the grimace thinking of her brought on.

"Yes, that right there. What's that face about, son? Are you not excited about the new job anymore?"

"No, I am. Well, I think I am? I don't know. I'm not really sure what I'm doing anymore, Mom."

"Ah, so the girl did give you another reason to think about staying then, didn't she?"

I looked at my mom, wondering how in the world she knew about the fallout with Blaire. Could she read my mind tonight as a weird Christmas party trick?

"Come on, Cole. Give me a little credit. I did raise you. You've never caught feelings before, and this is a new level of melancholy, even for you."

She took a sip of her wine.

"And also, Austin told me the real reason you canceled on dinner last week, not the whole 'you got caught up at the festival' as you claimed."

I felt my cheeks redden slightly to be called out by my mom for canceling dinner with her for a girl. Remind me to murder Austin later.

"Oh, it's all right. Tom invited me to watch a Christmas movie marathon at his place that night, so I was able to accept the invitation. I told you, I love our weekly dinners and I'll miss them, but I've got Tom in my life now, so it's not like I'll be sitting around lonely and waiting for you to call. Now, what happened with the girl?"

I sighed. I guess this was happening.

"We just weren't compatible, I guess. She's from Holly Ridge, I'm from Winterberry Glen. She loves Christmas and I hate it. I tried to *fix* her by going behind her back and trying to arrange a job for her at the capital. I'm leaving in a little over a week. It never would have worked, anyway."

My mom looked at me in silence, the lights from the tree reflecting off the wineglass as she moved to set it on the table. Oh boy, she was really settling in to lay it on me.

"You know, Cole. Those are some reasons to keep people apart, but the only one I heard you can't change is where you were both born. You don't *have* to take the job with the state just because it was offered to you and it was part of your plan. You can apologize for being a bone-headed mansplainer and be better in the future. And I've seen more Christmas spirit in you this year than I have since you were ten years old, the last Christmas your dad was here. Christmas spirit doesn't happen just because you decide you like a holiday again. It's about the joining of a community to celebrate the act of giving and being together, that sometimes miraculous things can happen if you just believe in something bigger than yourself. You've always tried to fix your problems by either growing a hard shell around yourself or by running away from them. I understand why you did both in the past, but you let Blaire and Christmas in this year. Hell, you've even let me in more with the talks we've had about our feelings and our past this month. Maybe it's time to think about facing your fears and your past head on, instead of running away and leaving it behind because it seems like it would be easier."

Mom let me sit there for a moment and digest what she had just leveled at me, content to gaze at her tree and into the kitchen where Tom was clinking and tapping away, putting the finishing touches on dinner. She had just picked her wineglass back up and was taking a sip when I found my voice again.

"It doesn't really matter where we're from, anyway. I got the call earlier this week. It doesn't look like the festival is going to make enough money to save Holly Ridge. There won't be a Holly Ridge this time next year. It just makes the most sense for me to move on and move up, taking the state government job."

My mom looked resigned that I wasn't quite ready to stray from the path I had been setting up all these years.

"Well, if that is the case, and that would be a real shame, then I would think Winterberry Glen might need its CFO more than ever, and this area is going to need strong, concerned citizens like your Blaire to see them through the transition. You could start new traditions, together."

Visions of Blaire and I starting new traditions, both in our towns, and as a couple, as a family, flashed through my head. They were the happiest Blaire thoughts I'd had in days, even if I knew they would never be true. My mom's next words barely broke through my thought fog.

"And anyway, I am of course sad to see a town lose its charter but, I think it might be for the best. I've heard rumblings about how the City Council isn't just inept but are crooked as well. Any way they can line their own pockets instead of the town's, they would take it."

That set me on an entirely different thought process. Barney said the numbers from the City Council's office looked like the festival wasn't going to make enough money, but the numbers Blaire had set up to auto send me daily—and hadn't canceled after our fight, her name popping up in my inbox sending stabbing pains into my chest every morning—were even better than her projections. I hadn't looked closely at the numbers since before the parade, too lost in my own head to do so, but was it possible that the council's numbers were wrong?

"Oh no, I know that look. That's your 'I need to go spend some time with my numbers look.' First, you're going to spend time figuring out the equation of how three people are going to eat seven fish courses, then we're going to watch *It's a Wonderful Life* while we digest. The numbers will still be there tomorrow."

At that, Tom popped into the living room, his Christmas apron still tied firmly around his waist.

"Dinner is served, Thomases!"

"It smells great, dear. We can't wait to dig in."

Mom got up from her chair and went to the doorway, reaching up to peck a kiss on Tom's cheek. I watched him gaze after her, matching the swoony look Mom had earlier. Mom was right. The numbers could wait. It was a long shot, anyway. Our family was changing, and for once, change felt right.

Chapter 30

Blaire

I had continued to avoid my family, trying not to let on that the festival likely wasn't going to succeed in saving Holly Ridge and also how sad I was about losing Cole. It was an emotional minefield inside my head these days, and not at all how I usually felt in the lead-up to Christmas Eve.

Christmas Eve was usually my favorite. Things were different now that the twins were old enough to have personalities and opinions, but they still believed in Santa, so their excitement made the whole night extra special. We would have a family dinner, just the seven of us, at my parent's house, making all the traditional Greene dishes, like cornflake cheesy potato casserole *and* mashed potatoes. We were a potato family, okay. There would be Mannheim Steamroller playing in the background, the wine would be flowing for those old enough, and it was an atmosphere that wasn't replicated any other time of the year. But this year, I couldn't even enjoy it. Sure, I was putting on a smile and laughing at H&H's antics, but my Christmas spirit had definitely left the building. I was pretty sure I had been successful in faking it, though.

In the living room, *It's a Wonderful Life* played on the TV on mute while Christmas music played quietly in the background. A fire was roaring in the fireplace with our stockings hung from the mantle above it, and I sat in my favorite chair with a glass of white wine. The rest of the family was in the kitchen and family room, either cleaning up from dinner or trying to tire the twins enough so they'd go to sleep with minimal fight when they got back to their house.

Gretchen and Dad entered the room, a glass of red wine and a hot toddy in hand, respectively, and sat on the couch. They sat in silence for a second before Gretchen broke the silence.

"All right, Blaire. This is the mopiest Christmas you've had since you found out the truth about you-know-who from Betty Perkins on the bus on the last day before break. What's going on?"

Okay, I guess my faking it still needed a little bit of work.

"Oh, nothing major, just tired from all the work on the festival, I guess."

"Try again, Blaire Bear," my dad said gently. "Do you know something about the outcome of the festival, and that's why you've been hiding over the past week?"

Damn our special father-daughter connection.

"We won't know anything for sure until after the Gingerbread Ball," I hedged, looking between their expectant faces, realizing they weren't going to let me get away with just that. "But it doesn't look good."

They looked at each other and seemed to decide Gretchen would speak next.

"And how are you doing with that?"

Something inside me snapped, like a fragile candy cane.

"Not great, Gretch! I have worked all my life to be enough for something, to be more than the former mayor's daughter, more than perfect Gretchen's sister. To stand on my own feet, without anyone else taking credit for my accomplishments. You both have such successful lives, great relationships, perfect children. How was I supposed to live up to that? I love to plan and make lists and

I loved the festival as a kid, dreamed of planning it, so that's what I did. I planned festivals with the goal of coming back here and planning the best damn festival Holly Ridge has ever seen. And then they threw in the whole *save-the-town* element and I thought to myself 'Perfect! Here's my own personal Greene family legacy!' But now, I haven't saved the town, I haven't planned the perfect festival, and once again, I'm here on Christmas Eve, alone, as the eternal seventh wheel."

Gretchen and my dad blinked at me in shock. They were so used to me running on the positive side of the emotional spectrum that this swing to the negative and admittedly self-deprecating was out of character for me.

Gretchen again entered the fray first.

"Did you know that being a lawyer wasn't my idea or my dream? At some point in time, people just started suggesting I would be a lawyer when I grew up. Maybe it was my grades, or the way I would argue loopholes and points, but suddenly, it was just assumed this was the path I should take. It's worked out and I'm okay with where life took me, but I never had the guts or passion to tell life where I was going to go like you do. I see you, Blaire, at these festivals and I can tell how fulfilled you feel with where you've plotted out your path. I'm sorry you've felt compared to me your whole life. We can blame the small-town, little-sister dynamic for that. But I have never believed that you wouldn't be something all on your own, something that you achieved through your own hard work and fortitude."

I sat and digested that for a moment. I had never known that being a lawyer wasn't Gretchen's dream. In that moment, I felt lucky that no one's expectations had shaped what I wanted. They had only made me work harder to get to where I wanted to be.

"You know, I always regretted I didn't do more to try to bridge the gap between Holly Ridge and Winterberry Glen when I was mayor," Dad said slowly. "A feud that started over something as silly and simple as a misdelivered Christmas tree. Half of my job as mayor was just listening to individuals complain about or disparage Winterberry Glen and the people that came from it. It's something that really wears on you after a while."

"Wow, Dad. Definitely sounds like you have some melancholy to work through too, but maybe we should let Blaire have this moment?" Gretchen said, taking a big gulp of her wine.

Dad laughed gently.

"It is related to the moment, I promise. I was just thinking that maybe the way to save Holly Ridge isn't to dread a partnership with Winterberry Glen, but rather to embrace it."

That got the wheels turning in my head.

"You might be right, Dad. Not everyone in the town would go for it right away, but if the towns were able to work together, it may mean that Holly Ridge and some of our traditions would be able to carry on, even if a merger has to happen. It may be time for a grand gesture."

Dad nodded his approval.

"And that would be something no Greene, and no one from Holly Ridge, has ever done before."

"Grandpa, can you come into the kitchen please?!" Hollis yelled from the next room.

Dad took the last swig of his drink and stood up. "Duty calls," he said, walking out of the room to see what sort of Christmas emergency needed his attention now.

Gretchen remained on the couch, looking at me intently, seeming to wait until Dad was out of earshot.

"As for your seventh wheel comment, come on, spill. What happened with Cole?"

I felt the flame that had lit in my chest at the thought of another avenue to try to save Holly Ridge flicker and go out at the mention of Cole's name.

"Cole? That was nothing. Just some moments that fizzled into absolutely nothing."

Gretchen put on her "I'm the big sister and I know best" face, rolling her eyes and obviously not believing me.

"Maybe try again, Blaire. Susie may be a steel vault when it comes to town gossip, but even she cracks open when she's worried about one of her own. She told me he was looking for you a few days ago, that you came back down from the apartment separately, and he looked pretty crushed. So, what happened?"

"Oh, you know, the usual. Girl meets boy, girl and boy hate each other, hate turns into heated attraction that leads to some pretty potent physical chemistry, boy doesn't believe in girl and tries to solve girl's problems for her, and then boy is moving away and there was never going to be any longevity there anyway. So, what does it matter? It wasn't real."

Gretchen smirked as she sipped her wine.

"Wow, you've got it bad."

"What? No, I don't. If anything is bad, it's him for trying to get me a job with the state to plan festivals and—"

"Oh, he wanted to get you a job at the place he was moving to, so you would no longer be under a state contract that says you can't be together and instead have a chance to continue what you started? Yup, that's really horrible of him."

"Well, what about the fact that he hates Christmas *and* Holly Ridge?"

"You mean he hates them so much that he willingly spent additional unnecessary time with you at a Christmas festival that takes place in the very town he claims to hate?"

Leave it to Gretchen to cut right through the clouded vision I had of Cole's actions and shine the light on a different perspective. Damn lawyers. And damn Susie for not living up to her reputation of not gossiping around town. She must threaten to ban people from Jitters if they reveal their source.

"Sounds like maybe Winterberry Glen isn't the only one who deserves a grand gesture."

Gretchen stood from the couch, apparently content to blow up my way of thinking and then just leave.

"We're not going to solve thirty years of sibling strain and negative thinking tonight, but please let me know how I can help with both the festival and Cole. I think it's time I lived up to the

Greene legacy you and Dad have both set by helping Holly Ridge be the best it can be."

With that, she walked into the kitchen, and I heard her collecting her kids and husband, ready to head home for the next stage in their Christmas Eve plans. I knew it would be a long while before I was ready for visions of sugarplums dancing in my head. I had some work to do, and only a few days in which to do it.

Chapter 30.5

Austin (8:06 p.m.): Dude, when were you going to tell me about this Gingerbread Ball thing? It sounds like a great way to ring in the New Year.

Cole (8:15 p.m.): The Holly Ridge Gingerbread Ball? Why would I tell you about it? It's the end of the Christmas festival, but no one from Winterberry Glen ever goes.

Austin (8:22 p.m.): That's not the case this year, man. From the sound of the chatter at Muggsies last night, sounds like it's going to be a packed house this year. Maybe if you left that office of yours, that you don't even work in anymore, you'd know these things.

Cole (8:23 p.m.): I've had some things to finish up. Speaking of, I need to send one more e-mail, and then I'm locking this place up for good. I need to catch you up on some stuff. Grab a six-pack and meet me at my place for the West Coast tip-off in 30?

Austin (8:25 p.m.): Color me intrigued... I'll see you then.

To: BWindfall@stategov.gov
From: CThomas@winterberryglen.gov
Date: December 29 8:33 p.m.
Subject: Important Financial Update

Dear Mr. Windfall,

I'm sorry to bother you during the holidays, but I have to imagine if you're anything like me, you're not quite capable of keeping away from the e-mails and numbers during the end of year time. I've had a look at the Holly Ridge financial sheets after something wasn't sitting right with me, and I think there are some things you need to see. I've attached some documents, with a summary upfront, but it may be helpful to talk things through. I'm available anytime.

Best wishes,
Cole Thomas

To: CThomas@winterberryglen.gov
From: BWindfall@stategov.gov
Date: December 29 8:59 p.m.
Subject: Re: Important Financial Update

Dear Cole,
How right you are, my boy. The ding of your e-mail was a welcome distraction from the family shenanigans occurring in my house at the moment. I'll need to take a closer look at your attachments in the light of day, but I can see what you're concluding here already. Let's talk in the morning, say nine o'clock?

Best,
Barry

Charlotte (9:06 p.m.): According to my inside Winterberry Glen sources—also known as their romance book club—there is great interest in the Gingerbread Ball. No one knows if ALL government officials, past or present, will be there though...

Blaire (10:07 p.m.): That's great! An exact head count isn't necessary, but it's good to know they're interested in the invitation.

Charlotte (10:08 p.m.): You're sure you're not interested in counting one head in particular?

Blaire (10:09 p.m.): Who knows if he's even still in town. He may have moved to the capital all ready to ring in the new year in his new life. But if you do get any updates?

Charlotte (10:10 p.m.): You'll be the first to know.

Chapter 31

December 31
   Blaire

Growing up with my dad as mayor, it gave me a behind the scenes look at a lot of different town happenings and traditions, but the one thing that had remained a mystery in my childhood was the Gingerbread Ball. Held every year on New Year's Eve, the twenty-one and over conclusion to the Christmas festival was shrouded in glamour and mystery to my childhood eyes—though I did make a killing babysitting on New Year's Eve as a teenager for parents who wanted to attend the party. This year, we had transformed the community center into something unrecognizable, but the cloud of anxiety over how my overture to Winterberry Glen would play out dimmed some of the glamour the decorating committee and I had worked hard to create in the usually bland space.

I made my way through the door about an hour after the party had officially started, having not been able to get away much before go time to get home, shower, and change. As my eyes adjusted to the darkened room and I took in the room full of people, I noticed a lot of familiar faces from Holly Ridge, but almost as many unfamiliar faces from Winterberry Glen. Before I could stop myself, I started searching the crowd for one face in particular, one that was burned into my mind's eye.

"He's not here yet," Charlotte announced, coming to stand beside me and handing me a glass of champagne, which I gladly accepted, taking a swig to calm my nerves.

"But a lot of people from Winterberry Glen are here, which is good news," she continued. "I mean, the room could definitely use some mingling exercises," using her chin to point at the groups of townsfolk who had separated themselves into clumps of their own, "but at least the room isn't split down the middle?"

I nodded.

"Yeah, I'm glad they at least decided to accept the invitation, but I wonder how we could get people to mix it up without making them feel like they're at the first day of summer camp. It is a party, after all."

"Did someone say mix it up and party?"

A handsome man who looked vaguely familiar appeared on Charlotte's other side, his dark blond hair doing that intentionally messy look only men's hair could do and his hazel eyes twinkling with what I could only call mischief.

"I'm Austin, the better looking half of Cole and Austin, best friends since grade school. Thanks for extending the invite to our town for this shindig, Blaire. Are you and your friend here noticing the clumping problem this party has as well?"

His familiar face made sense now. I recognized him from a picture Cole had on his desk in his office. I remember staring at it when Cole was being insufferable last spring, wondering how the stick-in-the-mud behind the desk ever left it long enough to attend a baseball game. Now I understood the dynamics of their friendship. With just one sentence, I could tell Austin was one of those people it was almost impossible to say no to.

Charlotte held out her champagne glass to clink Austin's beer bottle.

"Her best friend's name is Charlotte, and yes, I was just saying that there seems to be some mingling resistance running through the crowd."

"Well, Charlotte, I think one way to combat that is for you and I to hit the dance floor, see if we can't lead by example. It's our duty as the best friends to these two power players, don't you think?"

Charlotte glanced over at me like she was uncertain about leaving me alone, which pulled my attention off the door, where I was watching to see if anyone else had joined us. A beat too late, I just laughed at her and waved my hand, gesturing them toward the dance floor at the front of the room. "Go, have fun, encourage some inter-town mingling. I need to work the room and get ready to officially welcome everyone soon too."

My eyes met Austin's and I saw something like compassion take over the mischief in his eyes.

"I told him he'd be an idiot not to be here. And his favorite color is red, so he'll be doubly rewarded when he listens to me."

With that, Austin put his hand on the small of Charlotte's back and steered her toward the dance floor. Glancing down at my red party dress, I smiled slightly to myself, glad that I had gone a bit out of my comfort zone to wear the dress Gretchen and I had picked out of her closet last night when I realized I didn't want to wear anything I had of my own.

I made my rounds, full of mixed emotions, to see so many of my neighbors and friends in one room on what could be the last Gingerbread Ball in Holly Ridge. I also recognized some of the Winterberry Glen faces, including Mrs. Krazinsky back in the community center without her service dog. Apparently, she antic-ipated feeling much calmer this go around than she did at the town hall meeting last spring. I spotted Louise and her husband from the Old Coach Inn standing near the DJ booth, enjoying a cocktail and swaying to the music. I was glad they had taken me up on the comped tickets I sent over after the snowstorm.

I stopped and made small talk, but I couldn't tell you anything that was said, between keeping an eye on the door for

Cole, yelling at myself internally for keeping an eye on the door, and going over the remarks I needed to make soon, I was just a bit preoccupied. It seemed like maybe Cole wasn't going to come after all.

I walked past the dance floor, where it appeared Charlotte and Austin had been somewhat successful in getting folks to break with their packs and join them. Charlotte was talking with someone I recognized from the government center in Winterberry Glen and Austin was charming Ethel, probably earning himself a free pie in the process.

I looked at my watch and realized I couldn't put off addressing the crowd any longer, so I went up to the DJ and nodded at him, letting him know I was ready to use the mic when the current song ended.

The song trailed off softly and I took a deep breath, realizing this may be the last time I'd get to address the crowd as the Holly Ridge festival planner.

"Hi everyone, and welcome to the Gingerbread Ball! Even though the main stretch of the festival is over, and we have to wait another year for Christmas to come around again, this has always been one of my favorite events of the whole celebration and I'm so glad to see you all here tonight. I especially want to welcome our neighbors from Winterberry Glen for changing their plans somewhat last minute and joining us here tonight.

"The reindeer in the room that no one is talking about is whether or not there will be a Holly Ridge this time next year. We won't likely know that for sure for a little longer yet, but what I realized with some help over the past few weeks is that it's a mistake for our towns not to form a partnership, whether it's forced by a change in city limits or not. Christmas is all about coming together with your neighbors to celebrate and share in the good things in life and to give back to your community. I think our community will be stronger if we embrace all our neighbors.

"I know I haven't been alive as long as this feud has been going on, and just because some festival planner says so doesn't mean all those bad feelings will disappear overnight, but I do know that this year's festival was better because someone from Winterberry Glen was involved in the planning. I believe in the power of the Christmas spirit, so I don't think there's any better time to embrace a new path forward than at the start of a new year."

For the second time in just a few weeks, my eyes suddenly caught Cole's from the back of the room. I couldn't take the time to parse all the emotions that were pouring out of those brown eyes and not lose it on this stage in front of all these people, but a warmth bubbled up inside of me just knowing he was there.

"It will be midnight before we know it, so be sure to grab a drink to raise a glass to the new year. I hope we'll toast to a new future for our towns and a wonderful year ahead. Thank you all for a fantastic festival. It has been a life-fulfilling dream having the chance to plan something for all of you to enjoy."

I noticed applause coming from all corners of the room, but I couldn't stop myself from making a beeline for Cole at the back of it. I came to stop in front of him, drinking in his perfectly fitted suit, the way the jacket hugged his broad shoulders and the tailoring accentuated his tapered waist. I almost wanted to duck behind him to see how those pants hugged his ass, but got caught in his gaze, a shy smile on his face as he greeted me.

"Hi."

I smiled.

"Hey," I responded back.

"You looked great up there—and you look beautiful. I love your dress."

"Told you!" Austin exclaimed as he and Charlotte bustled behind us, making their way to the bar to grab their toast drinks, Charlotte laughing at his antics, making it clear their path through the room was not the most direct, so they could eavesdrop on us.

Cole laughed.

"I see you've met Austin."

"I have. He told me he told you you'd be an idiot not to come tonight."

"He did. And he was right. There was just something I had to wait on first. Do you want to go take a walk?"

I nodded.

"Let me just grab our coats," he said, putting his hand on my lower back, just close enough to my ass that it felt possessive, and I felt something in my chest slot into place.

Cole

I hated watching her cover up that dress with her long black pea coat, but I was hoping this wouldn't be a short conversation, so I wanted her to be warm, and it started to flurry outside while I made the drive over to Holly Ridge from my house. I hate that she doubted I would be here, but I had to wait for a courier delivery before I could leave for the party.

We walked in strained silence for a few steps, both of us unconsciously heading for the town square as soon as we exited the community center. I decided I should be the one to start since I suggested the walk in the first place.

"So, I see a whole lot of Winterberry Glen folks at that party."

Blaire nodded.

"I realized that telling everyone out right that Holly Ridge was going to lose their charter would be a huge mood killer but thought that we could start the year off on the right note by suggesting the town embrace the merger instead of dreading it. Obviously, I can't force Winterberry Glen to spend their money a certain way, but I thought if they were invited in and introduced to the festival, they might want to carry on some of the traditions next year, just so the area doesn't lose out on such a great opportunity. I'm just mad I didn't think of this earlier. The towns could have been celebrating together all festival long."

She took in a breath.

"I also know this doesn't make up for what happened to you as a kid, but I hope it would stop it from happening to anyone else. I know you probably think it's silly for me to think Christmas spirit has that much power over human behavior, but I don't know, I think it at least opens people up to listening more than any other time of the year."

This woman. I knew I needed to stop running from my past and face my own issues with where I was from and the damage I had let the feud cause me, but even after I had hit her weak spot and walked away from her, she was still willing to put in the work to do what she could to help heal me.

We reached the steps of the gazebo and both stopped, staring up at the snow. The flakes reflected from the tree lights and the gazebo, shimmering and glistening, as they fell to the ground.

"That does mean a lot to me, Blaire. I think you'll be able to make a lot of progress during next year's festival in having Winterberry Glen embrace the Holly Ridge festival traditions."

It was hard to keep a straight face as Blaire whipped her head to look at me, once what I had said sunk in.

"Wait, what do you mean 'embrace the Holly Ridge festival traditions'? There won't be a Holly Ridge this time next year?"

"Well, that's why I'm late. I was waiting for this to be delivered."

I pulled the January first edition of the capital's newspaper out of my jacket's inside pocket and handed it to her. Blaire unfolded it slowly, and I watched her take in the headline.

"I don't understand. You told Tanya that the money wasn't there, even from the first week. Numbers stayed steady and increased a little bit after Tanya's follow-up piece on the parade, but—"

I decided to put her out of her misery.

"I was talking to my mom on Christmas Eve when the wording of the call I got from Barney hit me. The numbers they were looking at were from the City Council, which means the council wasn't just forwarding your reports to the state. I looked closely at the reports that had come from you and realized that if the state was looking at those numbers, there was no way they would have been able to make a call that early in the festival. I got the City Council's reports from Barney and compared the spreadsheets. There was money missing in the City Council's reports. The state had provided me with budget numbers for the past few years so I could prepare for overseeing the festival's financials, so I dug into those reports, too. The City Council has been stealing from Holly Ridge basically since they took office. The numbers they were sending from the festival were false. They had some really good finance guys on their payroll to bury the signs, but well, I'm better, and I found their trail."

Blaire blinked at me.

"So, Holly Ridge isn't being dissolved?"

"Not at all. The state still wants someone to work with Holly Ridge to get the numbers back on track and be sure that no one is left behind who was in on the council's scheme, but they're not going to punish the town for the vendetta of a few individuals. I actually think heads are rolling in the state's audit office for not catching this sooner. They offered me a promotion already."

Blaire's eyes, which had been shining with excitement, dimmed at the reminder that I would be leaving the area and went back to looking at the newspaper in her hand, avoiding my gaze.

"Oh, that's so great for you, Cole. I'm glad they're rewarding your skills so early on."

"Blaire," I said, waiting for her to look back up at me. "I didn't take the promotion. I'm actually not taking the first job they offered me either. I'm staying here."

"To oversee Holly Ridge's finances through the transition?"

"No. They did ask, but it came with a no fraternization clause I wasn't willing to continue upholding."

Blaire blinked at me. Gosh, she was beautiful.

"So, you're staying? And not working for any government bodies? And Holly Ridge will remain a town and continue to have a festival?"

"That's right. And I also want to apologize for trying to fix a new job for you. It wasn't because I didn't think you could get it on your own or that you needed my help. It was because I wanted the chance to be with you, for real, without any sneaking or hiding, and I saw an opening and didn't think."

At this, Blaire threw herself at me, her mouth finding mine and warming the part of me that had gone cold since I walked out of that studio apartment last week. My arms found her waist, pulling her tight to my body, my cock going rock hard the instant I had her back in my arms.

Blaire slowly drew back for air, keeping her arms around my neck. I didn't loosen my hold on her, not wanting to have her farther from me than absolutely necessary but wanting to let her say what she needed to.

"The financial fortitude was hot enough, but the self-reflection and actualization was irresistible. And I'm sorry too. I should have let you explain where you were coming from, I shouldn't have written us off because of where you came from, or the fact that you were leaving. I have my own things to work through when it comes to feeling the need to earn things on my own."

"Maybe we can get a two-for-one therapy deal somewhere in town," I joked.

She groaned, the vibration carrying through her body to mine and making me grip her tighter.

"Who knew therapy talk would work so well for me?"

We both laughed, but then I grew serious, brushing a strand of hair out of Blaire's face and looking into her eyes.

"I'm serious, Blaire. I want to make this work. You carried me through this Christmas season I thought would be my last in my hometown and made me realize I don't want to run anymore. I can't wait to see what else we can face together, and maybe sometime I can carry you through something you're going through."

Blaire's eyes started to well with tears when we heard a loud, and united, countdown coming from the direction of the community building.

"10, 9, 8—"

"To new beginnings?" Blaire asked.

"And to new traditions," I answered, bringing my mouth back to hers just as the crowd inside the center yelled, "Happy New Year!"

Chapter 32

March, the following year

Blaire

I walked up the stairs to city hall, still wearing a blazer, but that was one of the only things that was the same as the time I took this walk last year. When I entered the main hall, I didn't have to avert my eyes from one side of the entryway. Agatha, Arthur, and Rudolph's photos had been removed right about the time they were arrested at the airport trying to flee to the Cayman Islands.

Somehow, Tanya had received an anonymous tip they would be on a flight that same day and the authorities caught up to them at the airport in exchange for allowing her the exclusive on the story. That was Tanya's transition for her blog from small-town fluff pieces to more investigative and in-depth stories about local governments and financial scandals, with Cole coming on board to do the financial interpretation and combing through public records, seeing what other trails he could find. Her streaming show had been put on hold, and I heard they were taking a more true crime spin with it. Cole was in absolute heaven over his new gig.

Cole was one of the biggest reasons I had a spring in my step this morning. I talked about getting an apartment and finally moving out of my parent's house after we knew my position as Holly Ridge festival planner would be a more long-term appointment, but I ended up moving in with him last month instead. I mean, with those Jacuzzi jets in his tub and the way he knew how to use them, who could blame me?

A look at my dad's picture back on the wall as Holly Ridge Mayor pro tempore made memories of this morning's tub time fly straight out of my head. The state asked him to come out of retirement and step back into the mayorship until a special election could be arranged for the town to decide whether they wanted to go back to a mayorship permanently or keep the city council structure and then hold elections to fill those positions. Dad was willing to do so, but was adamant he wasn't putting his name on any ballots. I knew he missed his woodworking and might even miss having Holland and Hollis around on a regular basis.

"Good morning, Blaire," Larry greeted me from his seat at the top of the short flight of stairs just inside city hall.

"Morning, Larry! Did everyone beat me here today? I'm running just a little bit behind."

Larry's eyes twinkled knowingly.

"You've got a rambunctious crowd in there today, Blaire. Mrs. Krazinsky and Bucky came in talking about how they didn't understand why their idea of hosting a live Twelve Days of Christmas walk-through on the main street of Winterberry Glen got such poor reception last time and they were definitely going to bring it up again today."

I laughed, thinking about the presentation they had given last week about permits for twenty-three birds, plus the cows, for a new Winterberry Glen hosted event for the Christmas festival, only to be met with a lack of enthusiasm, even from their fellow townspeople.

"Thanks for the heads-up, Larry. Sorry in advance if you're now singing the song all day."

I walked down the hall, continuing to laugh at Larry's warbled, "Fiiiive gold-en riiiiings," from behind me.

That's right. I put my money where my mouth was and created a combined committee from both towns to help plan the Christmas festival this year and going forward. It meant more spaces to do activities, a larger volunteer base, and we'd be able to do a Polar Express for the first time this year, since there were train tracks that ran on the other side of Winterberry Glen. The feud wasn't going to be forgotten overnight, but I think we took a giant step forward to bringing our two towns together, and I was proud of the work we were doing on the festival, even if it was a bit chaotic. We were calling it the Holly Ridge-Winterberry Glen Holiday Festival this year, because we just didn't have the time to come up with a new name. But we're holding a contest for suggestions, because I only wanted my mouth full of a few select things on a regular basis and that name was not one of them.

Right as I put my hand on the doorknob to open the door to the conference room where all this fun was waiting for me, I heard my name from behind me.

"Blaire! Hi! So glad I caught you!"

Gretchen approached from the other side of the hall. When my dad was asked to become Mayor pro tempore, he asked Gretchen to come on board as the town counsel and she agreed. Turns out our talk on Christmas Eve wasn't just transformative for me, but Gretchen decided she wanted to be a lawyer for something she cared about, not for a private firm that was going to pay her the most money.

"Hi, Gretch, I'm running a little late. What's up?"

"Just wanted to be sure we were still on for lunch today. You hung up on me sort of abruptly this morning before I could confirm and didn't answer my texts."

I mean, you'd hang up on your sister too if your hunky boyfriend came back into the room, stripped off all his clothes, started filling the tub wearing nothing but his glasses and gave you *the look* from the doorway.

"Oh yeah, sorry about that. Cole needed me for something. Yes, lunch today is perfect. See you at Joe's at noon? I gotta get in there."

Waving goodbye to Gretchen, I opened the door and was greeted by, "No, a group of swans on the ground is known as a bank, it's in the air that you call them a wedge!"

I smiled as I stepped into the chaos, because while it was chaos, it was Christmas, and it was home.

Tree Lighting Ceremony, Two years later
Cole

It was the third Christmas tree lighting since Blaire had taken the helm as festival planner, and in what was a surprise to no one, it was the biggest one yet. After last year's parking fiasco, the HRWG Holiday Festival—much to Blaire's chagrin, the name of the festival remained, though the acronym made things slightly less painful—created satellite lots over in Winterberry Glen and ran shuttles between the two towns. Word was that those satellite lots were even 75 percent full tonight.

Blaire and I had grown as a couple over the past two years, both of us seeking out therapists to work through our individual issues, and occasionally seeing one of our therapists together to work on our communication and strengthen our bond. That often meant that it was hard to hide from the other what we were thinking, like right now.

"Are you sure you're okay, Cole? You look a little grey. I'm the one about to go out there and kick off a Christmas festival, not you, you know."

I laughed weakly at Blaire's joke, mostly because keeping my plans for tonight a surprise over the past few weeks had been a serious challenge.

"I'm fine, Blaire. The cold must be getting to me tonight. I'll grab an extra hand warmer from your stash, and I'll be good to go."

"Okay, if you're sure."

The girl did not make it easy to surprise her.

We had been at the Old Coach Inn—Louise always made sure to give us the same room she did that first night two years ago—sitting in front of those picture windows wrapped up in the comforter from the bed, drinking from a bottle of wine and snacking on a charcuterie board Louise had surprised us with when Blaire led me to believe she knew I was planning to propose this Christmas Eve. She was right, of course. I knew a Christmas time proposal would be the best kind of proposal for Blaire, so I had it all worked out to do at her family's Christmas Eve dinner.

Even though after being in a relationship with Blaire Greene for almost two years, I was getting better at not being right all the time, this was one thing I wanted her to be wrong about. I didn't want her to see the proposal coming. That meant bumping up my timeline a bit and declaring my emotions, publicly and loudly, at the Christmas Tree lighting ceremony was the next best idea I could come up with. So yeah, I was feeling a little queasy. So sue me.

"I better get to the stage and meet this year's honorary tree lighter. I'll see you after?"

She pressed a quick kiss to my cheek and walked off, all business.

Right after she walked out of the gazebo, Austin walked up to me.

"Hey man, how you holding up?"

"Oh, you know, nothing like a little public declaration of emotions to the woman I want to spend the rest of my life with to make me feel alive," I responded.

"You're going to do great, Cole. She's going to love this," a female voice answered from the chest pocket of Austin's coat.

"Hi, Charlotte," I directed at the phone, which Austin pulled out to show Blaire's best friend on the screen.

"She basically threatened my life if I didn't call her right this second to be sure she didn't miss anything since she's still in DC until closer to Christmas," Austin answered by way of explanation. Charlotte nodded her head to corroborate his story on the screen. Apparently, having your best friends enter into a relationship automatically created some sort of bond, which Austin and Charlotte used with annoying efficiency to call both of us out when we were being stubborn about something.

"Okay, well, get both of you down into the crowd so you have a good view. Mom and Tom should be standing with the Greenes right down front, they're supposed to be saving you a spot, Austin."

"10-4, Mr. Thomas. We'll see you afterward!"

I took a deep breath and snuck my way to the back of the stage. The festival had grown so large and successful that Blaire had to hire a part-time assistant for the back half of the year to keep up, which was the only reason I was going to be able to pull this off. Melinda handed me an extra mic when she spotted me behind the stage, Blaire already having started her opening remarks, which meant it was almost go time.

"And now it's time to introduce this year's honorary tree lighter, Penny Cartwright!"

Blaire turned around to see Penny stepping onto the stage with me and threw me a look that was mixed with confusion and a little bit of anger that I was throwing off her carefully scheduled timetable. I figured she would forgive me for it.

"Hi, Blaire, everyone. Before Penny gets up there and does her thing, there's something I wanted to do first."

I walked up to Blaire and got down on one knee in front of her and both of our towns, plus several hundred other strangers.

"Oh my God," Blaire said, covering her mouth with her gloved hands. She'd stepped back from the podium when she saw me approaching, so only I could hear her. The crowd let out a gasp when they realized what was about to happen.

"Blaire Greene, you have made such an impact on our community over the past two years, taking the festival and making it more sustainable and inclusive, as well as inviting Winterberry Glen to be a part of the planning and hosting for the first time. The results for both towns are evident in the growth and success our towns have seen, plus there are a lot less brawls for the Sheriff offices to clean up. And while I have a new appreciation for my hometown, for me, that doesn't begin to compare to the difference you have made in my life. You've given me so much, helped me grow and have courage to face my past instead of running from it, and given me a love I never thought I would have in a million years. It's true love makes a fool out of you and you've made me a fool, but I've never been happier. Will you marry me?"

A speechless Blaire is something I've only accomplished a few times in our relationship, and this was one of those times. I stood, which seemed to wake her up, and she nodded and said aloud, "Yes."

At that, I dropped the mic and gathered Blaire in my arms, laying a kiss on her that probably wasn't appropriate for a family-friendly event. Penny's secret cue for throwing the switch on the Christmas tree was Blaire saying yes, which must have happened, because the crowd's cheers and applause only seemed to increase in the seconds after Blaire gave her answer, but I couldn't see anything beyond the woman in my arms. I ended the kiss, hugging her tightly to me, my hand cradling her head as I picked her up and spun her in a circle, unable to stay still because this wonderful woman had agreed to be mine forever. I put her back on the ground and we looked out into the crowd, at our families and friends, beaming back at us from the front row. I don't think I could ever have the appreciation for Christmas that Blaire did, but it absolutely meant something to me now. I looked over at Blaire to find her looking back at me. I knew at that moment it didn't matter where we came from or what the town we lived in was called. In this woman, I would always find my home.

This book came out of a love of reading, a love of Christmas, a love of love stories and a whole lot of support and cheerleading from friends and family. I can't believe it's out here in the world.

The first thank you belongs to Dan, for putting up with and being so supportive of this dream that got inside my head and just wouldn't go away.

For my URL to IRL friends and all of Bookstagram, when I say I couldn't have done this without you and your support and excitement, I mean it. Allie and Izzy, you both deserve medals for receiving and acknowledging my anxieties, quelling my fears, and cheering me on the whole way. Kelly, thanks for still loving me through my Oxford comma journey. To my Literary Devices Book Club Admin babes, Merry Cockmas and thank you for your love and support, and to the rest of our LDBC friends, I'm so glad to have shared this past year of reading, learning, and laughing with you all.

To my Real Housewives of Meadville and Sarah and Kelsey; you've supported me from near and afar, you've never questioned why and have never been afraid to tell that your "friend wrote a book." Thanks for celebrating all of life's moments, both big and small. Maria, thanks for the long-distance movie date and the texts that started it all.

Lacey, I know I can honestly say this book wouldn't have gotten done without you, and I know it wouldn't be what it is today if you hadn't been a part of the process. You give the best homework assignments, ask the most insightful questions, and just made this book better. Thank you. (And a shout out to Steph for bringing us together.)

Dad, you got the dedication, but I am who I am because of you. I know this leap scared you, but you never let it stop you from supporting me, asking me to explain acronyms (sorry for switching careers just when you got a handle on the Higher Ed stuff) and always checking in on how the book was that day. Writing an absentee dad for Cole was hard because I have the best in the biz.

To the Panera Breads of Northern Virginia: many pages of this book (including some of the steamy ones) belong to you.

And to you, dear reader, thank you for taking a chance on a debut indie author who loves Christmas, corny jokes, Taylor Swift, and love stories. You made this dream possible. I hope I brought you some joy in return.

About the Author

Rachel grew up in Western PA and found her love of reading early in life, supported by her parents with frequent trips to the library and local bookstores. She stumbled into the online bookish world in late 2020 diving headfirst into the Romance genre. In 2021, she changed careers and took a job at a bookstore and started her first official novel-length writing project.

Now Rachel is getting an MFA in Popular Fiction at Seton Hill University and juggling too many story ideas for one brain to handle. She's excited to continue to share Happily Ever Afters with you that bring the laughs and the love.

When not immersed in her bookish world, you can find Rachel hanging out with her husband and two cats, spending time with friends in the Washington DC area, and rooting for Pittsburgh sports teams.

Also by Rachel Holm

HOLLY RIDGE SERIES

Carry Me Through Christmas

Coming Soon: Make You Mine This Christmas

THE BRANDT BROTHERS SERIES

Capitally Matched

Capitally Engaged

Capitally Unexpected

Coming Soon: Capitally Yours